LIKE A WINTER SNOW

A PORT WILLIS ROMANCE

LINDSAY HARREL

To the lovely readers who asked to return to the quaint village of Port Willis—this one's for you. <3

A romantic Christmas story set in beautiful seaside England? Yes, please! Lindsay Harrel's *Like a Winter Snow* is the perfect mix of depth and charm. Joy and Oliver are so likable and relatable—and together, they're just plain adorable. Plus, I can't help but love that they're a little older than your average hero and heroine.

From the Christmasy atmosphere to moments both swoony and poignant, I loved this story...and I know readers will, too!

Like a Winter Snow offers all the depth of emotion Lindsay's readers have come to expect from her books—wrapped up with a wonderful Christmas bow! A beautiful story of learning to let go of the uncontrollable and opening your heart to love. I highly recommend!

CHAPTER 1

*I*f it were anyone but Sophia Barrett getting married, Joy Beckman wouldn't dream of getting on a plane tomorrow.

She stepped from the elevator onto the polished laminate flooring of one of the top skilled nursing facilities in New Port Richey, Florida. At least if she had to leave town, she knew that her mom was getting the best care possible while recovering from her broken hip and subsequent surgery.

"Rockin' Around the Christmas Tree" played softly from a speaker as Joy made her way toward her mom's room. She flashed a smile at the few residents in wheelchairs she passed in the hall, her insides twisting at the way their faces lit at the small kindness. How she wished she had time to sit and talk with each one, especially those whose families didn't live nearby. Any time of year, that would have gripped her, but especially now—no one should be alone at Christmas.

Still, all her focus today was on Mom. Joy had been dreading saying goodbye for the next two weeks, but it was time. She prayed the pep she was about to force into her voice would be enough to fool her mother.

Of course, if it were one of Mom's bad days, it wouldn't matter.

"Knock, knock." Joy peeked her head through her mom's open doorway. The room was small but comfortable, with pale blue walls and several framed garden photos bursting with pastel colors. An essential oil diffuser in the corner dispensed a lavender scent throughout the room.

Mom's nurse, Linda, blocked Joy's view of the bed as she took her patient's vitals. She looked up at Joy's greeting. "Good afternoon, Dr. Beckman." She kept her drawling voice low.

Joy approached the bed and finally spied her sleeping mother, tucked in and looking so frail under a bright pink and yellow quilt she'd made years ago. Betty Beckman had once been as vibrant as the colors in the quilt, with thick brown hair that gleamed, high cheekbones, and green eyes that had always hinted at some secret joy within. Now, her gray hair hung limp around her shoulders, combed and neat but lacking its former luster. Her cheekbones protruded from her thin face. She'd lost so much weight just in the sixteen months since she'd received her Alzheimer's diagnosis.

And then there were her eyes. Instead of looking at Joy like the light of her life—the miracle baby Betty had been given forty-two years ago after so many losses—she sometimes viewed her as a stranger.

Joy cleared her throat. "I've told you, Linda. You don't have to call me Dr. Beckman. Joy is fine." Though she'd once taken such a thrill at the title bestowed upon her when she'd received her PhD more than ten years ago, her work in counseling women from all walks of life had ended when she'd sold her practice in Arizona last year and moved here to help Dad care for Mom.

She'd made the right call then. Was she making the right call now, traveling so far away a week and a half before Christmas to perform maid of honor duties?

But the plans were made. Her flights booked. And Sophia was counting on her to help with some last-minute details. Joy couldn't abandon her best friend.

Then again, she was needed here too. She'd already failed her parents once. And potentially doing it again . . . not an option.

"All right then, Joy." Linda finished her observations and draped her stethoscope over her neck. The plump woman angled a look at her. "I hear you're leaving town for a spell."

"Yes, for a wedding." Had Dad told her, or had Mom had one of her lucid moments? "How is she today?"

Linda's brows knit together. "Her recovery from surgery is going well, though it will most likely be another two to three weeks before she's released. As you know, it was a bad fall."

Joy tried not to let the words bring a sense of utter devastation, but no matter how hard she fought, they bulldozed her heart. Because if only she'd been doing her duty instead of sleeping . . .

No. Negative self-talk did no good.

She straightened her spine. "And her memory? How's that been today?" Joy sat in the chair next to the bed and took Mom's wrinkled hand, running her thumb over two veins rippling across the top. Mom's simple one-carat circle diamond winked from her ring finger.

"You know how it is. Good moments mixed with the bad. She was telling me about your trip, and when I asked a question about your friend—Sophia, is it?—she suddenly didn't know who I was referring to."

"Sounds about right." Joy had counseled several women through the loss of parents after dementia and Alzheimer's had consumed their loved ones' minds, so she'd known what to expect from the progression of the disease. But her heart hadn't been prepared to experience it herself.

Working to control the tears beginning to gather in her eyes, Joy blinked quickly then changed the subject. "I expected Dad to be here."

"He left, maybe an hour ago or so. Went to lunch but said he'd be back in a jiffy." Linda gathered a few empty containers of Jell-O and plastic spoons from Mom's movable bedside table and tossed them into the small trashcan under the nearby sink. "He told me about the assisted living facility he's considering. I told him I know many patients who live there and love it."

"What are you talking about?"

Linda's cheeks paled. "Oh, dear. I . . . never mind. Please forget I said anything." She started for the door.

"Linda."

The nurse turned, frowning. "I figured you knew. I shouldn't say anything else. Talk to him about it. But . . ." She studied Joy. "Get all the facts before you form an opinion one way or the other."

Turning on her heel, Linda left. Joy slumped in her chair.

Dad was thinking of moving Mom into a full-time facility after rehab was complete?

She needed to talk to him. Now. Joy dug in her purse and pulled her phone from within, noticing a text from Sophia on the lock screen.

Less than thirty-six hours! Eek!

Joy dismissed the notification, unlocked her phone, and dialed Dad's number. It went straight to voicemail. When was the man going to learn to keep his phone turned on? At nearly eighty, Dwight Beckman hadn't seen the need for a cell phone, but Joy had convinced him of its necessity. After all, she had to be able to communicate with him about Mom twenty-four seven.

She shoved the phone back into her purse, hopped up, and paced.

Fifteen minutes of fretting later, her father walked in sipping on a fifty-ounce Big Gulp. "Don't worry, it's diet."

"I wasn't going to say anything." She'd learned to hold her tongue when it came to her diabetic father and his eating habits. All she could do was provide good meal options and ensure he regularly saw his doctor. And pray. A lot.

Dad lowered himself into the chair Joy had vacated, his belly hanging over his belted pants. He set his drink on the ground, wincing a bit at the movement. "Did you finish packing?"

"Yeah. I came to tell Mom goodbye, but she's been asleep since I arrived."

"We had a good chat this morning before she dozed off." He turned and gazed at Mom with the most loving eyes.

Once upon a time, Joy had dreamed of a love like

her parents had. Devoted despite heartaches. On the same page in all the ways that mattered. Individual and allowed to thrive in the areas where they were different.

But she'd come to realize that it wasn't the plan for her life. That, instead, she was meant to be a friend and helper to all. And she had found peace in her place.

Still . . . in times like this, when life seemed so fragile, it would be nice to share the burden with someone else. To have a shoulder to lean on. Yes, she had Sophia, but her best friend had moved to England more than a year ago after meeting the love of her life, William Rose.

And of course, Joy had God, who would never leave her. But sometimes, having a flesh-and-blood partner in life sounded appealing.

Appealing . . . but not likely.

"What did you chat about?"

When Dad didn't answer right away, Joy moved to the opposite side of the bed and pulled up a second chair. "Linda mentioned something about an assisted living facility."

He frowned and pushed his large plastic frames up the bridge of his nose. "She shouldn't have done that."

"She thought I knew." Mom stirred, and Joy lowered her voice. "Why didn't I know?"

But the answer was obvious. Dad didn't feel like

Joy could be trusted to help them anymore.

"Nothing is decided, JoJo." His voice softened at the use of his nickname for her. "Your mom and I are just evaluating our options." He fiddled with some papers on the side table. Pulling a brochure from the bottom of the stack, he held it out to her.

She reached across the bed and took it. The glossy cover read *Glenn River Assisted Living and Memory Care,* and beneath the title, several grinning elderly residents played cards around a table.

"At this place, we'd be able to live in the same apartment. Your mother would receive the elevated care she needs, and I could pay room and board until I get to a point where I need more assistance as well. They'd cook and clean for us and take care of all of our needs."

"But I do all of that for you." Joy couldn't help the tremble that had crept into her voice. "You want to leave your home?"

"You've done a wonderful job, and we couldn't be more grateful, but maybe it's time for you to get back to doing what you love."

All of his kind words couldn't erase the truth—Dad wouldn't even be considering this move if Joy hadn't, literally, fallen asleep on the job.

She set the brochure down on the quilt and eyed her father once more. "I *am* doing what I love—taking care of you guys."

"As I said, it's just one of many options we're

considering. I don't want you to worry about it. Go and enjoy your trip."

"Sure. Okay." She'd endure the time away for Sophia's sake.

And when she returned in two weeks, Joy would get right back to where she was supposed to be—helping Mom and Dad in the difficult days to come.

CHAPTER 2

A piercing squeal met Joy's ears as she exited the gated area of Cornwall Airport Newquay.

Following the group of passengers into the airport's main lobby, she raised up on her tiptoes to try to catch a glimpse of Sophia. Some days, being five two had its advantages. Today was not that day.

Finally, the person in front of her broke off to the left, and Joy had a clear view of the room just in time to see a pair of arms closing around her.

"You're here, you're here!" Sophia let go and pulled away, her grin carefree and strong.

Joy laughed. "I am."

"Did you have a good flight?"

"Long"—she exhaled some of the stress from her shoulders—"but good." She'd actually managed to sleep a bit on the long stretch from Tampa to

London—a miracle considering the man next to her snoring the entire way as well as her stormy conscience hurling accusations at her. The moment she'd landed, she'd called to check on Mom. Linda had chided her, said they'd take good care of her mother in her absence.

But would they? Could anyone care for a mom better than a daughter?

"So glad to hear that." Sophia wove her arm through Joy's. "Let's grab your luggage and hit the road. I can't wait to show you Port Willis."

Be upbeat, Joy. Don't ruin this for Sophia. "And I can't wait to see it." Joy was supposed to have visited last Christmas, but her mom had been worse than anticipated. Sophia had come to Florida instead nine months ago, and they'd spent a lovely week together catching up face-to-face.

They walked toward the baggage claim area, and while they waited for her bag to be unloaded, Joy studied her friend. Soft black waves fell to Sophia's shoulders, framing her face, including her bright blue eyes. As always, she was dressed stylishly but simple. Her white sweater fit her long, thin frame well, and she wore her favorite pair of comfy black slacks. She'd exchanged her usual flats for boots, and wrapped around her neck hung a soft yellow infinity scarf. Her best friend rarely wore colors.

At least, she hadn't before moving here—before

finally healing from an abusive past relationship and all the yuck that went with it.

Finally, the carousel started moving, and bags of all shapes and sizes whirred by until Joy spotted hers. When it moved close enough, she stepped forward and lugged the leopard-print suitcase off the conveyor belt.

Sophia chuckled. "That bag is so you."

Yes, with her blond bobbed hair and bright and mostly vintage clothing, Joy's style definitely contrasted with Sophia's. "Whatever do you mean?" Joy's laughter joined her friend's, shaking her long earrings to a tickle along her neck.

It felt good to laugh. The last year hadn't provided much opportunity.

Sophia led her through the doors of the small airport, and a strong wind nearly knocked Joy back against the door, leaving her cheeks tingling. "Whoa. It's a bit chilly out here."

"I warned you it'd be colder than Florida."

They high-tailed it through the parking lot.

"You said the average temp would be fifty degrees." A glimpse at the sky showed full gray clouds threatening to burst. Hopefully the weather would make a turn for the better on Sophia's wedding day.

Sophia clicked a button on her key fob, and the lights of a blue sedan flashed. She popped the trunk and slid Joy's luggage inside. "The operative word being 'average.' It's rained nearly every day this month so far. I don't know what I was thinking, having a wedding in December."

They both climbed into the front seats of the car. How strange to see the wheel on the right side of the car. Sophia started the engine, and heat began to pour from the vents.

Joy buckled her seat belt. "You wanted a Christmas wedding. The most romantic time of year and all that."

"Yeah, but the weather is the most gorgeous here in the summertime. At least, that's my favorite season so far. But maybe that's just because it's when I first moved here."

"And met William," Joy teased.

A small smile quirked at the corner of Sophia's lips. "That too." The lemon air freshener dangling from the rearview mirror gently swung as her friend pulled out from the parking lot. "Oh well. If it's overcast and gloomy on my wedding day, or rains all day, or whatever the case may be, at the end of it all, I'll be Mrs. William Rose and that's what matters."

"Exactly. And then you'll have a lovely ten-day honeymoon in Italy before William has to start the spring term." Given her love of books and that she owned a bookstore, Sophia marrying a literature professor was perfect.

"It'll all work out." Sophia kept her eyes on the

road, but despite her own tiredness, Joy didn't miss the tremble in her friend's lips.

"What's wrong?"

"Can't keep anything from you, can I?"

"No, and you'd better not try." Joy spotted a sign for an overlook. According to Sophia, Port Willis was only about a half hour from the airport, but once they arrived at the small village, she suspected they'd be overrun with "curious" neighbors and local gossips out to meet the newcomer. "Pull over here and let's talk."

"Bossy as ever, I see." But Sophia did as Joy had asked.

"As your best friend and maid of honor, I'm allowed to be." Not only that, but considering their nine-year age difference, Joy had always looked at Sophia as the younger sister she'd never had.

When they reached the lookout point and climbed from the car, Joy had to keep her jaw from dropping. The Gulf back home was beautiful in its own right but nothing like the view in front of her. They stood on a grassy bluff, and the ocean pounded the cliffs below so hard that water misted her face. The roar of the ocean was strong but not angry—a reminder that Joy was a part of this world but not its driving force.

She breathed in the fresh air and hunkered into her newly purchased neon orange parka. The pockets warmed her hands as she turned to Sophia. "Well? Spill."

Sophia folded her arms across her chest. "It's nothing big, really. Just stress, I think. Running a bookstore during the holidays and planning a wedding is just much more than I anticipated."

"Hasn't your mom helped?" Sandy Barrett was a well-known event planner who specialized in weddings.

"As much as she can, but there's only so much she can do from Phoenix. She doesn't have contacts over here, and she's busy with her own events. In fact, she won't even be out here until the day after Christmas because she has a major event on Christmas Eve that was already planned when we chose our wedding date. She offered to hand it off to another coordinator, but I insisted she keep the engagement for the bride's sake." Sophia rocked back and forth on her heels. "I've kind of regretted being so generous, though. There's still so much to do before the wedding, and I just feel like there's no possible way to get everything done in time."

"When is Ginny getting into town?" One of the other bridesmaids—and the groom's former sister-in-law—American Ginny Rose was now a culinary student in London. She'd been Sophia's first friend in Port Willis.

"This weekend. In time for the bachelorette party."

"I can't wait to meet her." Joy nudged Sophia with her hip and slid a hand around her waist. "And I'm here now, so just give me a list and I'll go to town."

"Really?"

"Of course. What did you think I came here to do? Lounge around and eat bonbons all day?"

"What is a bonbon anyway?" Sophia's arms came around Joy once more and she squeezed. "I don't know what I'd do without you. Seriously. Even though I love my life here, I've missed you so incredibly much."

"I've missed you too. Life has been . . ." Joy quieted as thoughts of her mother, her father, and assisted living facilities spiraled through her mind. But she was here for Sophia, not to have a pity party about the direction her own life had taken. Her own failures. "So, now that that problem's solved—"

"Not so fast. I'm such a terrible friend. I didn't even ask you how your mom is doing. Just plowed ahead with my own problems. Please forgive me."

The smell of rain and wet earth tinged the air. "You have a lot going on."

"But you do too. So, how is she?"

Joy just shrugged. "About the same as the last time we talked. Dad is considering moving them into an assisted living facility."

"And what do you think about that?"

She didn't want to discuss this, or her guilt over leaving Mom would become evident. "I—"

A fat drop of water hit the ground in front of them followed by a hundred more.

They ran back to the car, ducking inside as fast as possible.

Sophia reached in the backseat and handed Joy a towel. "I've gotten used to these spur-of-the-moment deluges by now. I come prepared."

"Nice." Joy used the towel to dab her face and hands dry. "So, this list of last-minute things. Is it stuff I can handle on my own?"

Sophia's forehead scrunched. "Most of them, I think. It's just a lot of random little things that simply have to be done, like picking up the groom's gift I ordered for William, meeting with the venue coordinator to run through the order of events for the ceremony and reception, calling all of the vendors and confirming the details. But with this huge holiday sale I have going at the bookshop, I'm swamped with orders and trying to get them shipped out in time for Christmas. Not to mention working the front desk. My seasonal employee had a family emergency, so William's been filling in when he can, but . . ."

"Have no fear, friend." Joy handed her the towel. "Together, we've got this."

Yes, a to-do list was the perfect way to remind herself of why she'd come—and to justify leaving her parents to do so.

CHAPTER 3

No wonder Sophia was stressed.

Joy took the wedding to-do list in hand, stuffed it into her jacket pocket, and stepped out of Rosebud Books's front door. Despite the sun shining through a lightly clouded sky, the air whipped against her coat and gave her a reason to hurry. Still, she didn't want to miss any details of this small fishing village on the Cornish coast.

Port Willis seemed everything Sophia had described—quaint, with shops new and old lining the main thoroughfare, stunning views to rival the most breathtaking of locales, and affable townspeople who had come to greet their bookshop owner's best friend the moment they'd arrived in town the day before. But even more than its physical structure and residents, there was something remarkable about its essence. Somehow this centuries-old place that smelled of salt spray and fudge breathed newness into Joy's spirit.

"Hullo! Pleasant day, isn't it?" A male grocer tipped his head toward Joy then returned to tidying his display of apples and oranges in the wooden crates outside his store.

"It's beautiful."

Moving past Trengrouse Bakery and the local bank, she continued walking down High Street—or up, rather. The road led from one end of town to another, ending at the docks, which were currently behind her. Last night, Sophia and William had taken Joy to a favorite restaurant down that way, and afterward they'd stood on the short pier in the moonlight. Despite the cold temperature, there had been something soothing in the sway of the dock, the gentle rocking of the boats. And when William had slipped his arms around Sophia's shoulders, and her friend had leaned back against him, Joy's heart had nearly burst with contentment. How she had wished for such a man for her friend, who had suffered so much pain.

And now, to focus on helping her friend have the wedding day of her dreams. Joy shook herself from the memory and continued climbing the steep road toward the antique shop where Mrs. Mavis Lincoln was holding Sophia's groom gift for William.

Seeing the sign for the store, Joy hustled across the road and pushed her way through the door.

Instant warmth greeted her, as did Mariah Carey singing about what she wanted for Christmas. The upbeat but modern tune seemed a jarring contrast to the shop, which was stuffed to the brim with treasures from every bygone era. In front of her, a large wardrobe that reminded her of the one from those Narnia movies appropriately welcomed her into this other world. Surrounding that, knickknacks of all kinds called to her—everything from a stack of ceramic chinaware to mid-century chairs and a collection of antique purses, including one vintage beaded bag that practically screamed her name.

To her left sat an artfully arranged display of Victorian Christmas cards. Joy's fingers itched to flip through them. But no, she had a job to do . . .

Okay, a few moments wouldn't hurt anything.

She removed her gloves and stashed them in her purse then slid her fingers over one card with rounded edges and a now-faded but once-vibrant picture of Santa feeding grain to a flock of hunting geese. Flipping to the next card, she couldn't hold in a giggle at the strange illustration that depicted two large mice fighting over a piece of hard candy the same size as them.

As she held up the card to see it better, a small yip startled her into dropping it. Joy turned around to find a medium-sized white dog sitting on its haunches and staring at her. He wasn't menacing at all, just curious, his head cocked, one ear standing on end.

Joy bent slowly to pick up and replace the card in its case then knelt once more near the dog, holding out her hand, palm down. "Hi, boy. Are you the local guard dog?"

"More like lap dog."

Her head rose to find the owner of the British accent—and Joy nearly did a double take.

Behind the dog stood a forty-something man around six feet tall, with broad shoulders, a neatly trimmed beard, and rich brown eyes that reminded her of her favorite coffee beans. He wore a nice pair of dark blue jeans and a long-sleeved, collared shirt underneath a black sweater vest. On anyone else, his style would have appeared boring to Joy, but on him it seemed classy. "H-hi."

H-hi? Seriously? She was forty-two, not fourteen.

But when a woman saw a man who was a cross between Henry Cavill and Gerard Butler, apparently it rendered her unable to speak.

Especially when that man wasn't wearing a ring on his left hand. Yeah, she hadn't been able to stop herself from looking.

Don't be ridiculous, Joy. Focus on the dog.

Right. The dog. She swung her gaze back to the adorable little mutt, who looked at the man as if waiting for a cue. Finally, he sniffed the air then rose to approach. He was missing a back leg and hopped over to her.

"Oh my goodness, you are just the cutest, aren't you?" she murmured.

The dog bumped his head against her hand and she was a goner. "What's your name, sweetness?"

"Don't let him fool you." The man came closer and lowered himself into a squat.

The scent of his cologne—an Oriental mixture of cinnamon, vanilla, and something else she couldn't quite name—drifted toward her. Joy bit her lip to hold in a sigh of pleasure at smelling the extremely masculine and yet cultured fragrance.

Oy vey.

He continued. "His name is Rascal, and he owns it. He will steal you blind if you ever happen to leave your food unattended. Isn't that right, old chap?" As the man scratched between Rascal's ears, the dog's tongue lolled out.

"Well, I don't blame him. Dog food just isn't that appealing when there's a burger to be had, right, Rascal?" She ran her hand down his soft fur, the motion bringing pricks of tears to her eyes. It had nearly broken her heart to give up her dogs when she'd moved in with her parents, but she'd managed to find good homes for all of them.

At the man's lack of reply, Joy snuck a glance at him.

He studied her for a moment then cleared his

throat and stood. "Sorry he interrupted your browsing. Can I help you find something specific?"

Joy followed suit, brushing off a few strands of dog fur as she rose. "It's no trouble at all. And, actually, I'm here to pick up an order."

"All right. If you'll just follow me, I can get you squared away." He whistled and Rascal was at his side in seconds.

She followed as he threaded his way through the tiny aisles of the shop, finally arriving at a desk with a register.

The man pulled a stack of order cards from a box. Wow, old-fashioned—how appropriate for an antique store. "What name is the order under?"

"Sophia Barrett."

He looked up and a grin split his chiseled face. "Ah, the bride to be. It's a pleasure to meet you."

A laugh sputtered from Joy's lips. "She is indeed a pleasure to meet, but I'm not her." She offered a handshake. "Joy Beckman. The maid of honor."

Something twinkled in his eye. "My mistake. Oliver Lincoln." He took her hand and for a moment, she thought he might bend forward to kiss it.

She held her breath until he released his hold.

O-kay. Time to cut back on the BBC miniseries episodes, then.

Joy folded her hands in front of her. "Lincoln, you said? So, you're related to the owner?"

Oliver dug through the stack of cards. "She's my aunt. I live in London, but she's been having some health difficulties the last few months. Her gout is taking its toll, I'm afraid. Since I'm a groomsman in the wedding, I was already planning to come to town, so I decided to make an extended holiday of it to get my aunt back on her feet." He pulled a card from the stack. "Here it is. That took long enough. I've tried convincing her to upgrade to a computer records system, but she won't hear of it. I'll return in a moment."

As he wandered through a curtained door, Joy blew out a breath. A man who owned a three-legged dog *and* gave up time to help a sick aunt. Whew.

She absolutely, 100 percent could *not* mention this little meeting to Sophia, or Joy would never hear the end of it. No man had turned her head in . . . well, never like this. In her twenties, she'd been busy with school. She'd tried some online dating in her thirties but quickly decided that was not for her. One too many dates had spent the entire dinner whining about their exes, and Joy—therapist that she was—had helped them figure out the root of their relationship woes. Each time, they'd been back into their ex-girlfriend's good graces before dessert had arrived.

A long time ago, Joy had come to realize that singleness was her lot in life. And for the most part, she was actually okay with being everyone's friend. A helper to all.

So why was she reacting so strangely to Oliver?

"It must be the jet lag."

"What's that, love?" The man himself returned to the room just in time to hear Joy muttering to herself.

"Uh, nothing." And there she went biting her lip again at the way he'd called her "love."

Stop it, Joy. It's just something the English say.

She zeroed in on the item in Oliver's hands. "Is that the gift?"

"It is—and a nice one at that." He slid the rosewood case across the desk and popped it open to reveal an antique fountain pen.

"Oh, that's perfect for William. He's going to love it." Joy had spoken to Sophia's fiancé a lot over the last year—several times when Sophia wasn't around—so she could ascertain whether he truly had her friend's best interests at heart.

Every time, he'd passed her tests with flying colors.

"Absolutely." He snapped the box closed and placed it in a bag for Joy. "My mate sure does love his books and writing."

"How long have you been friends?"

"I grew up here in Port Willis before my parents moved us to London when I was in year eleven. William is five years younger and was friends with my brother Ben. But then he and I ended up at uni together when I was a postgrad student and stayed in touch even when he moved back here and I stayed put." Oliver handed the bag to Joy.

She did the math in her head as well as she could. William was thirty-six or thirty-seven, so that would make Oliver in his early forties. Just like her.

Move along, Joy. "That's wonderful. Friendships are everything." She took the bag from him, and her fingers brushed his.

Nat King Cole serenaded her from somewhere up high.

Oliver's eyes locked with hers. "Yes, they are."

A moment passed before she could eke another word past the lump in her throat. "So I guess I'll be seeing you around?"

"I hope so."

"Me too. I'm sure we will, with the wedding activities and such."

And as she turned to leave, one thought worked hard to poke through the romantic wall she'd built around her heart—friendships were important, indeed.

But sometimes, they weren't quite enough.

And other times, they simply had to be.

CHAPTER 4

"*A*nd this is the main street." Joy flipped the camera on her iPhone so her parents could see her surroundings. It was only 7:00 p.m. on a Thursday, but the streets were deserted, nearly everyone having gone home or into a pub for dinner.

Every storefront glimmered with an assortment of twinkle lights hung round their doors and framing their picture windows. Wreaths with red bows had been pinned to most of the streetlamps—the historical wrought-iron kind, with a hanging inverted cone of glass. The only thing missing was a blanket of snow, and Joy would have sworn she'd stepped into a town from one of those cheesy Christmas movies she secretly couldn't stop watching.

She maneuvered the phone to face the ocean

then toward a prominent hill overlooking the village. "Just up that way is the local lighthouse. It doesn't work anymore, but apparently it's open for the public to explore."

"Where did she go?" Her mom's voice drifted from the phone. "Why can't I see her anymore?"

Joy hit the reverse button on the screen and switched back to selfie mode. "I'm here, Mom."

"Oh, hon, I was just telling your dad that you'd disappeared." Her mother sat up in the hospital bed, her eyes clear. A good day after several bad ones, according to her dad's daily report.

And Joy was missing it.

She continued walking down High Street toward Sophia's cottage, located just behind the bookstore. Thanks to finishing up yet another item on her friend's to-do list, Joy had already been running late for dinner before calling her parents. But she couldn't stand going another minute without connecting with them.

"Sorry, Mom. I was just trying to show you the town. I'll take lots of pictures and send them to you. It's kind of dark now." The Cornish sunset was obscenely early in December—it began around four fifteen, with nightfall complete by five thirty or so. But tonight a heaven full of stars glittered above her, a thousand diamonds rejoicing in anticipation of Sophia's nuptials approaching in nine short days.

"That'd be nice, dear." Mom's voice started to drift, her eyes to dim.

No, stay with me. "I miss you guys. I'm so sorry I'm not there."

Dad poked his head into the frame. "We miss you, but it sounds like you are having a wonderful time."

"Wonderful time? Where is she? Joy? Honey? Why aren't you here?" Mom's wail projected from the phone and flooded the nearly empty streets—and Joy's heart.

"Mom . . ."

"We're going to go, all right, JoJo? Talk to you soon." And with that, Dad hung up the phone, leaving Joy in the silence.

Her lips trembled and she shut her eyes for a moment, breathing in, out, deep, strong. There wasn't anything she could do for Mom from here but pray Dad could get her calmed down.

Joy pocketed her phone and increased her speed, feet aching as she walked downhill. Maybe her yellow T-strap heels hadn't been the most practical choice for a day of running errands in a town nearly as hilly as San Francisco, but they went so well with her black A-line pocket dress dotted with pictures of tiny cacti and tied at the waist with a large yellow belt. Accented by black leggings, a red cardigan, and dangling cactus earrings, the outfit was one of her favorites.

Too bad she'd had to slightly diminish its effect

by throwing her puffy parka on top, but Joy was smart enough to forego fashion for warmth when necessary, especially since they'd already experienced a dip in the temperature since she'd arrived two days ago. In fact, according to Sophia, temps would continue to decrease during Joy's visit. Meteorologists were even calling for snow around Christmas, which hadn't happened in fifteen or so years.

A door closed and a bell jangled somewhere nearby as she hurried toward her destination.

"Joy. Hey! Hold on."

She stopped so abruptly at the sound of Oliver's voice that a small smattering of loose gravel caught her unaware. Joy twisted on her heel and fell onto her rump. In moments, a wet tongue licked her face.

"Thanks, Rascal." She nuzzled the dog and looked up into Oliver's face—the one she hadn't been able to get out of her mind since she'd first seen it yesterday.

"Are you all right?" He offered his hand to her.

She took it, and he hoisted her upright. "Other than a little wounded pride, yeah. I'm good." Joy inspected her leggings and found a small hole near the ankle. She pointed to it. "I take it back. My day is ruined. I will never recover."

Oliver's lips twisted in humor. "You must allow me to buy you another pair."

Joy laughed. "That's sweet, but these can't be replaced, unfortunately."

"They're that expensive?" His question wasn't one of concern, just curiosity—not surprising, considering his blue sport coat looked as if it cost a pretty penny.

"No, they were probably two dollars at Goodwill. But it's the memories surrounding them that can't be replaced." Like when she and Sophia bought them and tried to have a *Sisterhood of the Traveling Pants* moment . . . and they'd been more like long shorts on her friend. Oh, how they'd laughed.

Or the time when she'd spilled salsa on the leggings during a recent movie night with Mom. Joy had chosen *You've Got Mail,* one of Mom's favorites, and they'd curled close together on the couch until her mother had fallen asleep.

Yes, that was a memory she'd be going back to over and over in the coming months, something to hold onto when the grief and trials seemed fiercest.

Hands in his pockets, Oliver leaned against a lamppost. "Your smile turned quite serious just then."

"I was just thinking about my mom."

His silence in response urged her to continue.

Huh. That was usually *her* tactic to keep clients talking. Funny thing was, she wanted to share her heart with this almost-stranger.

He was throwing her off balance in more ways than one.

It really was getting cold out here. She folded her arms across her chest to try to get warm. "I'm sorry. I'd love to chat, but I need to get going. I'm late."

"Are you heading to Sophia's by chance? Because so am I."

"Really?"

"Really." He eased off the lamp and started walking, whistling for Rascal to follow. "So if you don't mind the company . . ."

"No, not at all." *I'd enjoy it quite a bit, actually.*

Oh, brother.

Rascal flew past them. The dog navigated the steep hill just fine despite his missing limb, somehow managing much better than Joy in her heels. Her toes squished at the front of her shoes and burned.

"Can I assist you down the hill?"

How was it he'd noticed her difficulty but hadn't made her feel bad about her silly choice in footwear? This guy was racking up the points.

Points that meant absolutely nothing, because, well, she was leaving in ten or so days. And despite that it had already literally happened, she would *not* allow herself metaphorically to fall head over heels for the first time in forever—not with someone who was un-keepable.

But still. She appreciated his thoughtfulness.

"Considering I don't want to end up with a scraped face or broken limb just before I have to stand in front of a hundred people at my best friend's wedding . . . sure. Thanks." Joy took his arm and allowed him to support her down the hill. Her head only came to his shoulder, but their arms rubbed against each other as they maneuvered toward their destination.

Maybe she should pat herself on the back for selecting these shoes after all.

He's just being nice, Joy.

Right. Back to reality. Again. "So, you said you were in town to help your aunt. How is she?"

"She's doing a little better. Thanks for asking."

"Are you caring for her alone?"

"My parents are coming down after Christmas and staying for a few weeks, but for right now, I'm all she has. Which isn't much, I'm afraid. I don't know quite what to do other than ask her what she needs and fetch it for her."

"And help keep her business running." They passed a fudge shop and Joy inhaled. The smell of the chocolate wafted outside despite the CLOSED sign on the white door. "That's vital for a small business owner."

"As I well know."

"Oh?"

Oliver cleared his throat. "I own my business as well."

"Yeah? I used to own a women's counseling practice."

"Two peas in a pod, then, eh?"

She couldn't help the grin that overtook her at the old-fashioned idiom her mom used to say all the time. "What kind of business do you own?"

"An accounting firm."

"Oooh, yeah, so I don't think we're the same after all. I hate math."

"Pity. What was your favorite subject in school?"

"Does recess count?"

A guffaw rent the air. "You like socializing, do you?"

"I mean, I *did* choose a career where I listen to people talk all day, right?"

"I'm quite the opposite. If I could stay tucked away in my office all day long, I would. So long as I had Rascal with me, that is."

"He's such a sweetheart."

At that, Rascal stopped and turned then yipped in agreement. Oliver and Joy laughed.

"You're a dog person, I can tell."

"I used to have six dogs. Each one was a rescue next on the list to be euthanized before I took them home." She sighed, her joviality gone. "I may never have children, but those dogs were my babies. I couldn't bring them with me when I moved—"

"Moved?"

They reached the bottom of the hill. Oliver released her arm.

See? Just being a gentleman.

A breeze ruffled the bottom of Joy's dress, bringing a chill with it that left her shivering for a moment.

"I left Phoenix about sixteen months ago and moved to Florida to help care for my mom after she was diagnosed with Alzheimer's. My parents are seventy-nine and eighty, so it was difficult but necessary. And six dogs wouldn't have brought the peace my mom needs right now."

Oliver squeezed her elbow, and Joy was struck with the sudden desire to snuggle deep into his arms, to see if he'd be as warm and gentle as he appeared. "That's amazing."

"My parents are the amazing ones. I'm just blessed I get to be there with them."

He shook his head as if in disbelief. "I'm in awe and I barely know you."

"Don't be too impressed. Remember, I'm also the one who can't walk down a hill by herself. So . . ."

His eyes roamed her face. "I think I could learn a lot from you."

"And I'm sure I could from you too." She said it casually, though with his eyes searching hers, she felt anything but.

"Then ask. Whatever you'd like. I'm an open book."

She tilted her head. "Why do I get the feeling that's not always true?"

His strong jaw clenched as if she'd hit upon a nerve with her words. "It may not be always true, but it's true right now. You're easy to talk to, you know. Must be the therapist in you." Oliver paused. "Or maybe it's just you." The whispered words floated toward her on the breeze.

They stood under another lamppost outside Sophia's house, and the glow hid half of his face in shadow. The moment felt private, hidden . . . theirs.

She needed to lighten said moment. Now.

"I get that a lot." Joy forced a smile and pointed to Sophia's house behind them. "Shall we?"

"Indeed."

Rascal led them across the road, and when they reached the front door, Joy let them in. "Soph! Sorry I'm late."

Sophia's head popped around the corner. "Hey! Oh good, you found Oliver." Her friend's eyes lit with interest as she looked between them.

Busted.

Joy strode forward. "How can I help with dinner?" Once she was in the kitchen, she noticed William chatting with a red-headed man at the tiny table.

"You didn't think I actually cooked tonight, right?" Sophia leaned forward and pulled three pizza boxes from the oven.

"I know you better than that. But you guys could have eaten."

William and the man at the table stopped talking. Sophia's fiancé stood and walked toward them, stooping way down to give Joy a hug. "Hey, mates. Good of you to come." He adjusted his glasses before reaching over to slap Oliver on the back then slipped his arm around Sophia's shoulders.

The red-haired man stood as well, his jeans and hoodie making him seem underdressed next to Oliver and William, who was never without a collared shirt or sweater of some sort. "I don't think we've met."

"Ah, yeah, sorry." William ran a hand through his dark blond curls. "Joy, this is my mate and groomsman Steven Applegate. Steven, this is Joy Beckman, Sophia's maid of honor. And you know Oliver."

"Pleasure." Steven shook Joy's hand.

"Likewise. I've heard a lot about you."

"All good things, I hope."

"Of course." Joy turned and lifted her eyebrows at Sophia, whose lips twitched. Yes, good things, indeed. According to Sophia, Steven and her friend Ginny were perfect for each other but weren't in a relationship beyond friendship.

"How about we eat and talk? I'm starving. The bookstore was a madhouse today." Sophia kissed

William on the cheek then opened the top of the pizza boxes.

"I see you got a sausage and pineapple." Joy pinched Sophia's side. "Weirdo."

"She's not weird. Just unique." William winked at Joy.

"Toe-may-toe, toe-mah-toe." Joy snagged some paper plates from the counter, handing one to each person in the room. They all dug in.

William lifted his soda water in the air. "A toast."

"What are we toasting?" Sophia asked.

"Love—and all the unlikely places it can lead."

Everyone clinked cups and cans together.

Joy felt eyes settle on her. Lifting her head, she met Oliver's gaze.

"Hear, hear." He threw back his soft drink with abandon.

Even though she knew she probably shouldn't indulge the butterflies fluttering their tiny wings in her stomach, Joy smiled, nodded, and took a hefty sip of her drink.

CHAPTER 5

"Girl, he couldn't keep his eyes off of you the entire night." Sophia slapped a label on a box of books headed for London then scooted it aside to make room for another on the bookstore's front counter. "He's single, you know."

Despite the guys staying at Sophia's until eleven the night before, the two women had risen early and headed to the bookstore before it opened. Overnight, twenty more orders had come in for rare books—Rosebud's specialty—and Sophia was determined to get the local ones shipped in time for Christmas.

Joy rolled her eyes and ran her finger down a printed inventory list. "You're just in matchmaker mode thanks to your almost-wedded bliss." Finding the title she sought, she crossed it out with a Sharpie.

As she took a sip from her third cup of coffee, her

eyes roamed the store. Joy had never been much of a reader—movies and TV shows were her jam—but there was something calming about being here, in a place that honored story.

Classy Christmas decor enhanced the already peaceful feeling of the shop's cozy, small-town atmosphere. A medium-sized tree perched in the front window display, and books wrapped with large bows were stacked artistically underneath the lowest limbs. On the front counter to the left of the register, Sophia had placed a simple Willow Tree nativity—understated but in a place of prominence. The crowning touch was the continuous strand of fairy lights strung from bookcase to bookcase, creating a soft glow that hummed in the pre-dawn hours.

"That's not true. There was something there." Her best friend blew a strand of hair out of her face as she taped up a new box and set to carefully wrapping two books with frayed covers. "Don't even try to deny it."

Joy clutched the list of orders in her fist. "I'll be right back."

She whisked away from her friend's knowing gaze. Bookcases surrounded her, towering over her short frame. As she took another look at the list in her hand, jazzy Christmas music spilled from well-hidden speakers.

Joy wandered the bookshop's aisles until she

found the first book on the list. As she delicately plucked it from the shelf, an expanding ray of morning light drew her eyes upward to the large windows over the loft area, where customers flocked during business hours to study, chat with others, or simply enjoy reading. The rising sun streaked beams of light through the store, adding a new depth, a new perspective.

Things always looked different in the light.

Because last night, she might have actually agreed with Sophia about Oliver's eyes on her. She'd felt a warmth, like the soft glow of sunrise, from his gaze. When she'd look his way, there was this quiet connection between them—like he understood her.

Of course, this morning she felt nothing but foolish. How could he understand her? They'd met a grand total of two times.

With quick steps, she found two more books and hauled her load back to the counter, glancing at the clock as she passed. The shop was set to open in forty-five minutes, and after helping Sophia here, Joy had to make numerous phone calls to confirm vendors. Enough thinking. They'd better get cracking.

Sophia's hands waited by the printer to snatch a label as it slid out. "I didn't get a chance last night to ask how your parents are doing."

At least she'd changed the subject. Though a supportive friend, Sophia had never understood

Joy's acceptance of the single life. A few years ago, she'd even threatened to create a profile for her on an online dating site. Thankfully, Joy's stink eye had been enough to scare Sophia away from that scheme.

"Mom actually had a good day yesterday. So that was encouraging." Joy slid the books she'd collected onto the front desk then snagged the order list.

"Did they say anything else about the possibility of assisted living?"

"Thank goodness, no." Inspecting the order list, Joy grabbed the first corresponding book then slid it inside a mailer envelope. She located the right printed label and stuck it onto the front of the package.

"Do you think they're still considering it?"

The heater clicked on, whirring somewhere above them. "I hope not." She secured the mailer closed.

"Why don't you want them to move? I know you'll miss living with them, but. . . . "

"It's more than that. Why should they pay thousands of dollars to get the same care I can give?" She pushed away the nagging thought that the levels of care were not as alike as she wished she could claim.

That if her mom had been in a facility with constant professional attention to begin with, she'd never have broken her hip.

"But don't you think it may be good for all of you to have your own space? And for your mom to get some specialized care?" Putting down the book she was holding, Sophia rounded the counter and clasped Joy's hand between her own two. "You're wonderful, Joy, but you have a PhD in counseling, not medicine. And don't you miss working? You are so talented and you've helped so many people."

"Of course I miss working, but it's just not an option right now. I'm still helping others—my parents." Joy squeezed Sophia's hands and tilted her head, forcing a grin. "I've just found a different path, like you have."

"Yeah, but this path makes me come alive." Sophia's eyes roamed the bookstore, taking in the books, smiling at them like treasured friends. Her gaze rambled back to lock onto Joy, penetrating deeper than anyone else's ever could. "Yours . . . well, I think it may be breaking you. I know better than anyone how difficult circumstances can change us, but I worry that yours are dragging you down, and you won't fight it because you feel like you're supposed to go down with the ship."

Joy's lips trembled. "They're my parents."

"I know, friend. But this . . . I think maybe it's beyond you."

"No, it's *because* of me." The words popped out before she could stop them. Boo for Sophia and her insightful heart.

"What do you mean?"

Joy pulled away. She had to busy her hands. Now. She snagged the next book and started packaging it.

Sophia rounded the counter and worked alongside Joy in silence. Waited.

Her friend had experienced heartache Joy couldn't imagine, yet she hadn't allowed it to turn her bitter. She'd found a way through the pain, the mess.

And she'd allowed Joy to walk with her through it.

Why did Joy have such trouble allowing Sophia to do the same for her?

She picked up an old copy of *Sense & Sensibility*, brought it to her nose, and inhaled the musty-but-not-in-any-way-disgusting smell of paper and ink that had been forged with story. Sophia believed the written word could heal.

And Joy knew from experience the spoken ones could too.

"It's because of me that Dad wants to move Mom into assisted living."

Sophia's hands stilled and she turned toward Joy, eyes filling with her trademark compassion.

Joy took a breath and continued. "It was my day to be with Mom. Dad was exhausted so I told him to run errands, see his doctor, do whatever he needed to do. That we'd be fine." Joy's thumb ran from the bottom to the top pages along the open edge of the book in her hand.

After she was quiet for half a minute, Sophia tucked her hair behind her ears and softly prodded. "What happened?"

Joy set the book down again. "I guess I was more tired than I thought." Memories of that day flooded in, and the story flowed from her lips.

The terror she'd felt at waking from an unintended nap to find her mother vanished. The mounting panic when Mom was missing for one hour, then two, then five. The overwhelming relief at getting a call from the police that they'd found her nearly a mile away—but then the crashing weight of guilt when they told her that, just before being discovered, Mom had stepped off a curb.

She'd broken her hip from the fall and been scheduled for surgery the next morning.

Joy couldn't wipe away the remembrance of her mother's whimpers of pain in the following weeks as she'd recovered, of her mother's confusion over her physical limitations and surroundings, especially once she'd been moved into the skilled nursing facility where she now resided.

"Oh, Joy." Sophia's arms came around her, and her friend's tears dripped onto her neck. Or maybe those were Joy's own.

Finally, Sophia released her hold and snagged a box of tissues from under the counter. She pulled one out for herself and offered the box to Joy, who grabbed a tissue and wiped her eyes.

Her friend studied her. "Do you remember what you told me time and time again when I blamed myself for David's abuse?"

"That it wasn't your fault."

"Yes." Sophia balled the tissue in her fist. "And it's not yours either."

"It's different, though. This is my responsibility. My privilege. And I'm so afraid . . ."

"Of not being needed?"

"What? No." Joy paused. "Maybe. I don't know." She looked down at her hands. Little flecks of white tissue stuck to her damp fingertips.

"Joy, you're always taking care of other people. It's who you are. But you also need to take care of yourself."

How many times had she preached that same thought to her clients? Joy sighed. "I recognize that. But I have no idea how in this case. Doing one kind of negates the other."

"I can see how you might feel that way, but I think it's still possible."

"How?"

"First, by telling yourself the truth. Fight against the notion that you're to blame for all of this. Alzheimer's is an unfortunate part of life, and I can't imagine how hard it is to watch your mom and dad go through that. Is it okay to embrace the sadness of the situation? To be angered by the injustice of it?

Yes, of course. But don't take on guilt that you weren't meant to wear."

The ever-empathetic Sophia sniffled and her voice shook. "And second, maybe do something small for yourself. You could apply for a few jobs, just to see what happens."

"I don't know . . ."

"Well, I do." That stubborn lift of Sophia's chin reminded Joy a bit of herself when she knew she was right about something. "And I also know that we can't see all the doors opened to us if we aren't looking or only focus on the path we've set before ourselves. Look around, friend. Explore. See what's out there."

That seemed impossible. Still . . . "You're right."

"Yes, I am." Sophia's eyes sparked. "And I'm not just talking about a job, you know."

Of course she wasn't.

Visions from last night replayed in Joy's mind. Of Oliver watching her as she'd joked with Sophia. Of his quiet smile that communicated so much more than a loud laugh ever could. Of the way her stomach had bottomed out when he'd leaned down to hug her goodnight.

It'd been a quick embrace—that of a new friend— but it had nearly knocked her off her feet. Again.

There was no denying she was attracted to him, but how did he feel? And what did it matter? She was leaving here before the year was up, going back to her parents who needed her.

Her path *was* set and no amount of Hallmark-laced notions of romance would change that.

Joy screwed her face into an appropriate glare and tossed her tissue at Sophia's face. "Hey, I'm supposed to be the older, much wiser friend, remember? Stop telling me what to do." She winked then turned to snatch the mailing labels from the printer. "Now, let's finish up here, or you're never going to get all of these mailed today."

Her friend opened her mouth as if to say something then snapped it shut. Shaking her head, she joined Joy in packaging the last of the orders.

CHAPTER 6

Out here, her troubles seemed far away.

The ocean roared in her ears as Joy walked with arms outstretched, shoulders back—finally loosened. Her fingertips skimmed the tall brown grass as she headed up the hill toward the lighthouse that stood sentinel over Port Willis.

After picking up some peanut butter fudge from Betty's Fudge Shoppe for the bachelorette party the next night, Joy's feet—and, she supposed, her heart—had led her here.

Here, where the darkening sky of late afternoon met the grassy bluffs that boasted a picturesque view of the foamy Atlantic waters. Joy stopped and veered off the dirt path just slightly, stepping close to the cliff's edge and peering down. More white than blue, the water swirled close to the rocky land below.

Gray clouds rolled across the horizon, gathering

like soldiers ready to march. It looked like rain might find her again, but having lived in Arizona for fifteen years before moving to Florida, she welcomed the moisture, loved the way it fed the beauty of the land around her.

Wind whipped her short hair back and forth across the tops of her ears, rendering her bobby pins useless.

But the cold outside couldn't match the warmth inside her. The day had been a busy one, with all the calls she'd made and errands she'd run for Sophia, so she hadn't had much time to consider what her friend had suggested this morning at the bookstore. Now, though, she'd spent the one-mile walk from town to the lighthouse praying, seeking.

Sophia had always spoken of this place with reverence, saying it's where she'd first started to hear God speaking to her again last year. And Joy could believe it—here, away from the village, it was so quiet. Made it easier to listen. Easier to hear.

She still didn't have any of the answers, but maybe that wasn't the point.

Joy turned and continued her ascent toward the lighthouse. After the last rise, the land flattened and the lighthouse soared over her. The round tower structure jutted into the sky, the stark white calm of its bricks a contrast with the battering ocean that threw itself violently against the lighthouse's outer walls.

As she approached, she noticed a wooden sign hung on the bright red door. Squinting in the waning light, she read its carved words.

Port Willis Lighthouse
Open sunrise to sunset
The lighthouse is no longer in service, but exploration is welcome so long as you have a care.
Please mind your step and enter at your own risk.
Maintained by the Port Willis Historical Society

Eyeing the clouds, Joy frowned. She should probably hurry back to the bookstore before the storm broke—Sophia undoubtedly could use her help with the last few hours of a fire sale—but something pulled her toward exploring, just as the sign had suggested.

Her friend's words from this morning drifted back to her. Sophia was right—she *was* always taking care of others. Her heartbeat quickened just a bit at the thought of crossing the threshold into the lighthouse, of enjoying a few moments for herself.

Maybe just a quick looksie wouldn't hurt. Still, she should let Sophia know she'd be along soon. Joy dug around in her canvas messenger bag, pushing aside the box of fudge before she finally found her phone. She snapped a picture of the lighthouse and shot Sophia a text. Then, after shoving the phone back inside her bag, she opened the door and stepped inside.

The air felt like it'd been trapped inside a freezer for weeks and only just released. Joy hurried toward the winding stone staircase. The bottom step was chipped, and no handrail guarded visitors from falling, though only ten to twenty steps were visible from below before they curved and connected with two walls on either side. This place had to be at least a hundred years old if not more.

She walked the steps, which were taller than most conventional ones. They clearly hadn't considered short people when designing this lighthouse. Joy had to pause a few times when she got off balance from the strain of constant rising, but eventually the steps ended and a medium-sized watch room opened before her. Joy strode toward the huge window that seemed to take up the entire wall opposite the steps. From here, she could see tiny Port Willis nestled into the bluffs, its harbor outfitted with bobbing fishing boats of all colors and sizes.

As she turned her gaze toward the ocean, one large plink of rain turned into several and then hundreds within seconds. Waves rolled in from the outer rims of the ocean, higher than she'd seen in the three days she'd been here. Despite being encased in rock and steel and whatever else comprised the lighthouse, she heard the whistle and whine of the wind as it whisked between the cracks of the old place.

Joy placed her hand against the window, cold penetrating her skin. She closed her eyes and listened.

"Joy."

Her eyes popped open and she turned to find Oliver standing at the top of the steps, drenched. His thick hair that had been neatly gelled in previous encounters now hung limp across his forehead in curled brown strands. Water fell from his slick black jacket onto the floor where he stood, panting slightly.

"Oliver." Joy rushed toward him. "Are you all right?"

"Just a bit chilled is all."

That had to be an understatement. "What are you doing here?"

His lips curved into a grin even as a shiver seemed to overtake him. "Rescuing you from the storm . . . or so I thought. But here you are, by all appearances perfectly dry and content." He began to shrug out of his coat.

"Here." She unzipped her parka, slipped it off, and offered it to him before he could protest.

He folded his coat and placed it over a railing underneath the window. Amusement lit his features. "You don't think that will fit me, do you?"

"Well . . . it's better than freezing." Joy tilted up her chin in playful defiance.

"If I *were* freezing, that may be the case." He waved his hand up and down his body, causing her to look at his clothing for the first time since he'd taken off the coat. Totally dry. His jacket must have been waterproof. "But it was nice of you to offer."

"Oh. Right." Her cheeks flamed as she put on her jacket. "And it was nice of you to come find me. But how did you know I was here?"

"I was in the bookstore shopping for my aunt when Sophia got your text. I volunteered to make sure you got home in one piece."

He peered down at her, a look on his face she couldn't quite define, just like she couldn't define the twisting of her gut.

She was used to taking care of herself. And totally capable of doing so too. But having someone else looking out for her . . . she kind of liked it.

Joy shook away from his gaze and pivoted toward the window. "I appreciate it. I know I should have headed back when I saw the storm coming, but I couldn't resist coming up here. I'm glad I didn't miss this view."

Waves pounded against the window, joining the rain in a song with an irregular drumbeat.

"Cornwall is known for its epic storms. Storm watching is actually quite popular in the wintertime." He eased beside her at the window, and his presence filtered heat her way.

"Whenever we get a big storm in Florida, we have to batten down the hatches, as they say. We've only had to board up for a hurricane one time while I've lived there, but I was just thankful it fizzled out before reaching us."

Mom hadn't done well during that one. Her shrieks of terror still reverberated in Joy's consciousness.

"Not a good memory, I take it?"

Was she really that readable, or was he just that perceptive? Joy sighed. "No. My mother . . . well, it's just difficult to switch roles with her. Going from clinging to her strength to being the rock in the storm."

"I'm sorry for what you're going through." No platitudes, no advice. Just sympathetic words that did more to soothe her heart than he could know.

Her chin quivered and Joy exhaled. "She's always loved storms, my mom. When I was young, she'd come to my room and wake me in the middle of the night, get me all gathered up in blankets, and take me to this big picture window we had. The lightning would zing across the sky, and the thunder would rumble, and my mom would say, 'Look at how powerful our God is. You never have to be afraid of anything because there's not a lightning bolt he doesn't know about, not a drop of rain he doesn't allow to fall.'" Joy fought against the tears. "But guess what? I'm afraid."

Her hand flew to her mouth, trying to stop the words before they came. This was too much to share with someone she'd met only days before, wasn't it?

Oliver tucked an arm around Joy's shoulder, giving her a light squeeze. A steady heartbeat thrummed beneath his chest.

It felt even nicer than she'd imagined.

For just a moment, she allowed herself the comfort, to lean into his embrace. Her eyes tried to peer through the sheets of rain, but Port Willis had become a blur in the deluge. It was only her, Oliver, and this lighthouse.

A pocket of safety in the storm.

She continued. "The thing is, I've always been able to see that the bad things that have happened in my life were somehow blessings in disguise. I can logically recognize that the rain falls on the evil and good alike. Even that our perception of rain and lightning can be flawed. We see only the chaos and destruction, the inconveniences, the way they ruin our plans. But fire and water, they bring life too. Refining. Rejuvenation." Joy shook her head. "Still . . . this time, I don't think I want what God seems to have planned for my life."

Oliver squeezed her shoulders tighter, resting his chin on the top of her head, and they stood like that for seconds . . . minutes . . . Joy lost track. His steady breathing anchored her as the storm slowly abated.

Finally, he spoke. "'None of us can see the way forward in the fog. We simply must take the next step—'"

"And trust that the light will lead us where we need to go." Joy craned her neck up to see Oliver. "You know *The Fog Rolls In*? That's one of my favorite movies." And it was totally obscure, a film she'd stumbled across on cable one Saturday evening a decade ago. But the story of two best friends who fall in love and then find themselves on opposite sides of a war had grabbed her attention from its first moments.

"I don't even own a copy of it, yet I know every word." Oliver loosened his hold on her shoulders and looked her square in the eyes. "I can't believe you've heard of it."

"Same."

"That quote has always meant a lot to me."

She'd opened up to him but to ask him to do the same meant something different. As a therapist, she always felt bonded to her patients after she heard their stories. And she knew what she asked next might set her up for heartache.

But she asked it anyway. "Why?"

He didn't even hesitate in replying. "There have been times in my life when I didn't know which way to turn. Everything from relationships that led me away from God, to business decisions that I feared making. I lost my first business because of that fear. It took years to rebuild, and now I have dozens of employees who depend upon me to lead them. It's quite a responsibility and one I don't take lightly. One I don't always know how to navigate. But I've promised myself I won't allow fear to be the reason for standing still again."

His Adam's apple bobbed as he swallowed.

Good gravy. She was melting into a puddle of mush. Never in her life had she connected with a man in such an effortless way. In past relationships, it'd been like pulling teeth to get a man to open up emotionally, to share his heart—and it had certainly never happened this quickly.

What was going on?

She opened her mouth to respond to his vulnerability but thanking him didn't feel quite right. What she should do is ask him to go on because she sensed there was more he wanted to tell her.

But if she already felt this close to him after a few days, what would learning *more* about him, his thoughts—his feelings—do to her? Especially when they'd be going their separate ways in a little over a week?

Joy stepped back a bit. "Oliver, I . . ." She pursed her lips. "Thank you for coming here. And for listening. But we probably should be heading back."

Though close to setting, the sun had reappeared as if the storm had never happened.

Oliver frowned but nodded. He followed her down the steps and out the door, into the light.

As they walked back to town in silence, one question poked at her. Why in this moment did the sunshine feel almost more frightening than the rain?

CHAPTER 7

Sophia's guest room sat at the back of the tiny house, but Joy could still hear the door bell when it peeled out a jaunty version of "Jingle Bells," the music floating down the hall and under the crack of her closed door.

The bachelorette party was about to begin.

Joy took a deep breath and clicked the SUBMIT button on her laptop before she could change her mind. A confirmation popped up.

THANK YOU FOR SUBSCRIBING TO JOB ALERTS IN YOUR AREA.

Leaning back against the bed's headboard, she closed her laptop, balancing it on her outstretched legs. She didn't know where her attempt at moving forward would go, but she'd taken Sophia's advice.

And now, it was time to attempt to have some fun.

With a renewed sense of gusto, Joy pushed the laptop onto the soft padding of the pillow-top mattress and stood. A quick glimpse in the mirror confirmed her mustard-yellow, high-waisted cigarette pants and tucked-in chevron knit sweater hadn't wrinkled. Joy popped in her favorite pair of green hoop earrings and slipped on some red pumps before she dashed down the hall.

Sophia was in the kitchen with a tall brunette clutching a suitcase. An excitement brewed between them as they spoke in hushed tones.

The clip of Joy's shoes against the wood floors announced her entrance and both women turned.

The brunette, who wore a blue sweatshirt that read THE LONDON CULINARY INSTITUTE, broke out in a huge grin that lit up the room as she rounded the counter and dropped her suitcase to the floor. "Joy!"

Joy laughed, the woman's warmth contagious. "So nice to finally meet you, Ginny."

They hugged as if they'd known each other for years, even though they'd never met in person. But Sophia had connected them from across the ocean.

The bride-to-be threw her arms around them, creating a group hug. "I'm so happy to have you both here with me."

The hug ended and Ginny fairly bounced in her purple Chucks. "And I'm so glad to have that last course behind me."

"Are you almost finished with your program?

You're going to be a pastry chef, right?" Joy dug her hand into a bowl of pretzels she'd set out on the counter, along with other snacks essential for a girls night. They were just waiting for Mary—Sophia's third bridesmaid, whose family owned her favorite pub in town—and then they'd head to dinner and come back here afterward for a movie marathon. Joy and Ginny had wanted to do more for Sophia, but she'd said what she really wanted was a quiet evening with her best friends.

Ginny snagged a piece of fudge. "Yep. Just finished, actually, but I have a three-month internship that begins next month. Then I'm done and the sky's the limit."

"I'm so proud of you." Sophia threw her arms around Ginny. "Maybe once you're done with that, we will see you more often, huh?"

"I wish. That's when the real craziness will begin. If I can do what I want, anyway." Biting into the fudge, Ginny leaned back against the counter.

"And what's that?" The pretzel crunched in Joy's mouth, the saltiness coating her taste buds.

"I'd love to open my own bakery. I can have complete creative control. And I already have experience running a business." She shrugged. "It seems ideal, really."

"I've been trying to convince her to do it here. The Pottery Club next door to the bookstore is closing—the owner is retiring—and it'd be perfect."

Ginny fidgeted and reached for a napkin. "And that sounds amazing, really. I'm just not sure what my future holds, and I don't want to lock myself down." She wiped her fudgy fingers.

"And what you mean by that is . . . you don't know what's happening with Steven. Is that it?" Sophia poked Ginny's arm. "Because you promised you'd keep me apprised, yet I've heard *nada* from you on the matter since the last time you visited."

"And when was that?" Joy watched the two women, the ease they had together, and a sharp emotion ensnared her. Not jealousy, exactly. She was glad for them. It was more like wistfulness because Joy had to leave here soon but the two of them would be able to stay.

They had the world in front of them. They'd chosen their paths. Had been transformed by them. They were free.

Joy wanted that for herself but she shouldn't. Because that freedom might take her away from the two people who needed her most right now. And that was a high calling. One worthy of sacrifice.

The memory of Oliver's arm around her the day before at the lighthouse flitted through Joy's mind.

She nudged it away without hesitation.

"September." Pushing off the counter, Ginny sauntered to the couch—only a few steps away, being that the cottage was only a thousand square feet—and sank down onto its soft blue-linen cushions.

Joy and Sophia joined her in the living room, which was surprisingly absent of Christmas decor besides the tree in the corner. Sophia had likely used most of her personal decorations at the bookstore.

"I would have updated you if there were anything to say. Steven has come up to see me in London several times in the last year, and I've come here. And I don't know . . . I really like him. Like, I . . ." Ginny's lips screwed up on one side, brow furrowed. "I don't know. I may even love him, you guys. The way chocolate chips love cookie dough. But I've been so busy and honestly, I'm scared. He's not Garrett, but I don't want to make any of the same mistakes I made with him either."

Sophia reached over and squeezed her friend's hand. "You're right. Steven is *not* like your ex-husband. And you are not the same woman you were when I met you. You know your own mind, Gin, but you've got to move past the fear. He's a good man, and I'm pretty sure he loves you too."

"I know." Ginny tugged at her ponytail. "I'm spending some time with him and his family for Christmas, so we'll see how things go. Either way, I need to decide what I want to do. If I do move back here, I want it to be for me, not for him. Not this time."

Joy admired the strength she saw in the women

in front of her. "I think it's really wise of you to not rush things."

A weak smile ghosted across Ginny's face. "Thanks. And sorry, Soph, but to be honest, I've been dreading this trip a little bit. As much as I'm excited to see you and William tie the knot, I know Steven and I need to have a talk. And then there's the whole matter of seeing Garrett again. I'm guessing he'll have his new wife with him . . ."

At Sophia's nod, Ginny grimaced. "Of course, I completely understand. And I'm glad that he and William have reconciled. William *should* have his brother at his wedding, especially since both of their parents are gone."

"You could have said no to coming—I would have understood—but it means the world to me that you're here anyway."

"Of course, girl. You're my best friend and William was my brother-in-law for five years. I love you both so much." Ginny exhaled and straightened. "But enough about me. What's going on with you guys? How are wedding plans coming?"

As they discussed whether the color of the baby roses in Sophia's bouquet would match the tabletop arrangements at the reception, Sophia's phone buzzed. She read the text and frowned. "It's Mary. She's running late and will meet us at the restaurant. You guys ready?"

Ginny stood and popped another piece of fudge

in her mouth, swallowing quickly. "Do you mind if I freshen up a bit?" She eyed Joy and Sophia. "Next to you two, I look like a complete train wreck."

Sophia laughed. "You do not. But go ahead. We're in no hurry."

"Five minutes. Be right back." Ginny snatched her suitcase and took off down the hallway.

Joy stood and wandered back to the kitchen. Ginny's mention of chocolate chip cookies had made her hungry. She snagged a bag of "chocolate biscuits" —close enough—and pulled the tab along the top to open it. "I really like her."

"I'm so glad." Sophia followed her and climbed onto one of the kitchen bar stools. "You, Ginny, and Mary are my people. I couldn't do life without you."

"Yeah, we're pretty great, aren't we?" Joy scrunched her nose as she opened the cookies and offered the bag to Sophia, who waved it away, seemingly deep in thought. "What is it?"

Sophia's gaze focused in on her. "You were pretty quiet when we were talking."

"Just observing. Sitting back and figuring out how all the pieces fit together."

"Yeah, but other than when you're working, that's not you. You're always the first one to dive into a conversation." Sophia bit her lip. "Did we make you feel left out with our talk of love and relationships?"

"Soph, no. Of course not." Joy reached her hand into the bag, the plastic crinkling as she rummaged.

Triumphant at last, she pulled an unbroken cookie from inside and took a bite. Sugar danced on her tongue and she sighed.

"Are you sure? I know you always play it off as cool and independent, but don't you ever get . . ." Sophia shrugged.

"Lonely?"

"I guess. Maybe?"

Joy swallowed and licked the front of her teeth before she spoke again. "Look, I am really happy with where I'm at. I've told you that a thousand times—I've embraced the single life. Even like it. I have a lot more freedom to do what I want to do. Independence." The irony of what she'd just said slapped against her cheeks as the words tumbled out. But it was true, in a way. She wouldn't have been able to uproot her life and move across the country to be with her parents so easily if she'd had a husband, a family.

"And anyway, I doubt I'd be able to find a man who could put up with my idiosyncrasies. I'm set in my ways. I like to stay up late watching *Dr. Who* one night and *Pride & Prejudice* the next. I'm a strange mix of vintage and modern, and I like it that way. No man would be able to figure me out. And I'm not changing. So I think I'm better off as I am—everyone's friend. I'm good with it. Really."

The look that flitted across Sophia's face personified doubt. "And what about Oliver?"

"What about him?"

More cookies. She definitely needed more cookies. Her fingers snagged a few from the bag, and she shoved a broken one into her mouth.

This time, the chocolate tasted bitter.

Sophia hopped down from the stool, took the cookie bag from Joy, and lifted an eyebrow. "That's what I thought."

*E*ight in the morning was way too early to be up, especially after such a late night.

But Joy couldn't sleep. She padded in her bare feet from the guest room toward the kitchen, the wood chilling her toes. The delectable smell of coffee wafted down the hallway. Either Sophia was also awake or she'd set the automatic timer on the coffeepot.

Rounding the corner, she discovered Ginny nursing a mug of Joe at the counter. The woman slumped forward in her seat, frowning, staring out the small kitchen window. First light trickled in, dark enough to make Joy wonder if it was going to be another cloudy day.

She cleared her throat as quietly as possible.

Ginny's head shot up and pivoted, eyes wide. "Oh, Joy. Hey."

"Morning." Joy walked around the counter to the coffeemaker and pulled a mug from the cabinet above. "Did you sleep?"

"Not well."

Pouring herself a cup, Joy took a sip. Ahhh. Liquid clarity. "Any particular reason?" As for herself, she'd collapsed into bed at 3:00 a.m. after a huge dinner at Village Pub—an adorable nautical-themed restaurant—followed by two different chick flicks, lots of popcorn and cookies, and chatting until they were so tired they started mumbling nonsense and descending into fits of laughter unbefitting their age.

"Oh, not much. Just the whole what-do-I-do-with-my-life-after-this stuff."

"So, really minor then." Joy grinned and stood at the counter opposite Ginny's seat, leaning against the gleaming granite.

"Yeah." Ginny cocked an eyebrow. "Why are you up so early?"

"Kind of the same reason."

"Really?"

"M-hmm." After another sip, Joy told her about Mom and Dad, the potential of working again—she'd already received five job notifications in the last twelve hours—and even the guilt she felt over being away.

She started to say something about Oliver too then stopped. It wasn't the same as Ginny's relationship with Steven. Joy had no room to commiserate. It was ridiculous to even consider.

Because Ginny and Steven would end up together, once Ginny saw what the whole rest of the world saw—that Steven was crazy about her. He'd snuck up to their table last night during dinner to give her a hug hello and to kiss her cheek. The heat between them had sizzled more than the large stone fireplace crackling in the corner of the pub.

But Joy and Oliver . . . even if she wanted to explore that, it really could go nowhere.

Commiseration, no. Encouragement, she could offer. "You'll figure it out, Ginny. You are smart and capable and have an amazing man who supports you and wants the best for you."

A smile tugged at the corner of Ginny's lips. "You're right. Thanks, Joy. I'm so glad you're here. Be praying for me today, all right? I have lunch with Steven and his parents and afterward, we're going out to dinner. To talk."

Joy leaned close and wrapped her in a hug. "Absolutely."

"Aw, why are we hugging?" Sophia waltzed into the room, her black hair pulled back from her smiling face.

The two separated and Ginny laughed. "I just needed some therapy, and Joy was happy to oblige."

It *had* felt good, helping someone again. "I'm

always glad to listen." She turned to Sophia. "So, what's on the docket for today?"

Snagging some coffee and a chocolate cookie, Sophia sat at the eat-in table. "I was going to open the bookstore at ten for a few hours. I know it's Sunday and a lot of people don't venture out, but since it's the weekend before Christmas, I thought it may be a good idea to be available."

"Makes sense. What do you want me to do?"

"Actually, William offered to cover the store for me, sweet man. So I was thinking you and I could start packing up a bit around here?" After the wedding, Sophia was going to move into William's house since it was bigger. She hoped to rent her cottage in the new year when they returned from their honeymoon. "There's more last-minute stuff to do but the majority of shops will be closed around here."

"That sounds great to me."

"I'll help too until I need to leave for lunch." Ginny took a final swig of her coffee and hopped off the stool. "Besides, I've been dying to see your wedding dress, and it sounds like now is the perfect time for you to model it for us."

"Ooo, yes." Joy clapped her hands. "Great idea."

"It's a bit of a monstrosity to get into. I'll need some help."

"We can practice for the real deal."

Sophia bit her lip then squealed. "Six days until

I'm Mrs. William Rose. Can you guys believe it?" She stood. "All right, let's go see it."

They followed Sophia down the hallway to her bedroom, decorated in delicate whites, pinks, and greens. A floral quilt lay across the top of the king-sized bed, and a vase of silk pink roses adorned the white shabby chic side table. On Sophia's closet door hung a large white garment bag that nearly reached the floor.

Sophia lifted the hanger from the top of the door then placed the bag on the bed. A hot pink tag at the top declared the bag the property of S. Barrett.

Her friend glanced at Joy and Ginny, eyes sparkling. "Ready?"

"Girl, yes." Ginny wrung her hands in anticipation.

Sophia unzipped the bag . . . and gasped.

"What's wrong?" Joy stepped forward, certain she'd see some sort of stain marring the dress's fabric. But the white beaded bodice—rather low-cut considering Sophia's modest nature—and flowing Georgette maxi skirt appeared in perfect condition.

Yet Sophia shook her head, tears filling her eyes.

"Soph?" Joy pinched her friend's elbow.

Sophia jolted then pointed at the bag and its contents. "That is not my dress."

"What do you mean?"

"*My* dress has cap sleeves, a sweetheart neckline, gorgeous embroidery, and tulle lace. This"—she pointed again—"is not that." Her breathing grew ragged.

"Here, sit down." Joy helped Sophia lower herself onto the edge of the bed. "Just call the dress shop, tell them there's been a mix-up, and demand you get your dress ASAP."

"It's in London."

"So it's their mistake, right?" At Sophia's nod, Joy continued. "They can figure out a way to get it to you same day. And like you said, we still have six days to figure this out. It's going to be fine."

Sophia blew out a breath and unclenched the fists she'd started making. "You're right. Can you find my phone?"

Ginny located it on the dresser and handed it to Sophia. "Here."

"Thanks." Sophia found the shop's phone number and called, standing to pace while she waited. After a minute, she hung up. "It just kept ringing and ringing. No way to leave a message."

"Maybe we can tweet them or contact them via email," Joy offered.

"It's this little hole-in-the-wall shop, so I honestly don't know if they have a website. I was in London dress shopping when I happened across it." Sophia rubbed her forehead. "Should I just keep calling and hope that eventually the owner will answer?"

"That's not a bad idea. Let's start packing and you can call every ten minutes and pray you get through." Joy zipped the bag and waltzed to the closet door, eyeing it then turning on her heel. "Sorry, but unless you have a chair in here, one of you will have to hang this."

Ginny snatched it from her and replaced the dress where it belonged.

For the next several hours, the three of them packed Sophia's bedroom. Eventually, Ginny left and lunchtime faded into afternoon. Sophia's attempts to contact the dress shop proved futile, with Sophia growing more and more discouraged every time her calls remained unanswered.

Argh. Her friend did not need this—did not *deserve* this—especially after all she'd been through.

Joy's head spun with details of a forming plan as she dug into the back of Sophia's closet. She crammed a pair of black flats into a moving box. Reaching for sandals decorated with red jewels, she tossed them in as well and snagged some white wedges in the next breath.

"Something on your mind?" Sophia's voice piped up from her spot across the room.

Did her friend know Joy well or what? "I could drive to London and exchange the dress in person. Then we'd be guaranteed to at least know what's going on and get the deed done."

Sophia, who had been tossing piles of lounge shirts and sweats into a box, froze. "That's actually a great idea. But you can't go. You don't know how to get there."

"It's called GPS, silly. I'll be fine."

"But you'd have to drive on the opposite side of the road. It took me a few months to feel okay with that. And London is a five-hour drive from here."

"I've taken plenty of road trips." The thought of driving on the left was a bit nerve-wracking but nothing Joy couldn't handle. "I'd have to borrow your car, though."

Sophia bit her lip and turned once more to stare at the dress. "I should be the one to go."

Joy set down a pair of white ankle boots and walked toward her friend, placing a hand on Sophia's arm. "You have a bookstore to run and last-minute details that only you can accomplish. I really don't mind. I'm here to help. Let me."

"I'll call William and see what he thinks." Sophia got on the phone and dialed her fiancé.

While she did that, Joy stepped out of the room and snagged a few water bottles from the fridge. Uncapping one, she allowed the cool liquid to flow down her parched throat. Who knew one could sweat in the middle of a British winter?

Sophia emerged from her room a few minutes later and found Joy in the kitchen. She placed her phone on the counter. "William said there's snow in the forecast for London and its surrounding areas. It may be a bad storm. The forecasters aren't certain but road conditions could be sketchy. Neither of us think it's a good idea for you to go."

"But—"

"Alone, that is." Sophia tilted her head, worry evident in her eyes. "You can say no to this, Joy, but Oliver was there with William and offered to take you. He said his aunt was feeling a bit perkier and could handle the store for a day if you leave at first light tomorrow."

A whole day with Oliver? Alone?

She chided herself for the tiny thrill racing up her spine. A. Friend. He was just a friend.

A handsome, amazingly insightful friend who . . .

Stop it, Joy. Just . . . stop.

Joy must have waited too long to respond because Sophia shook her head. "That settles it. I'll just keep calling the shop and hope that someone answers tomorrow. It's probably closed for Sunday or something to that effect."

"Didn't you initially go there on a Sunday?" That was the only day Sophia ever closed the bookstore for part of the day.

"Yeah, but—"

"I'm going, Soph. You have to have your wedding dress. That's a nonnegotiable. And I for one am not willing to trust that the shop will get it here for you." She paused, mulling. "That's really nice of Oliver to offer to come with me. I guess, to be safe and ease your mind, I'll let him."

CHAPTER 9

Twenty hours later, Joy stood triumphant at the front of the wedding dress shop. In her hand she held Sophia's dress along with a two-hundred-pound refund.

Oliver followed her out to the car and whistled. "I can't believe the verbal thrashing you gave that woman—and all without yelling or saying one rude thing." He opened the back door to his silver SUV, took the dress from her, and set it inside with care. "That takes talent."

She rounded the vehicle and opened the other back door. "All I did was remind her she had a duty to her patrons to ensure they looked beautiful on their wedding day, and that it's a bit difficult for the bride to do when she doesn't have the right dress." Leaning in, she pulled the top of the garment bag toward her so it lay flat across the seat. "I still can't believe she didn't label the dresses more clearly. We're just lucky that Samantha Barrett hadn't picked up Sophia's dress and taken it to who-knows-where."

"Indeed."

She laughed at the simplicity of his reply. Last night, Sophia had said something about Oliver being on the introverted side, but with Joy, he'd never really seemed that way unless in the presence of other people. In fact, he'd been downright chatty this morning on the drive—during which she'd learned that he loved sushi but salmon (her favorite) revolted him, that he played a mean game of Yahtzee and dabbled in guitar strumming when he had a few spare moments, and that his ideal day consisted of walking and playing fetch with Rascal at Hyde Park.

When he'd asked about her, she hadn't known what to say. Even though she liked herself, she just didn't feel that interesting, not when most of her time was spent hanging out with her parents. So she'd gushed about her love of everything movie-related and confessed her secret addiction to the British royals—even that she'd stayed up all night when she'd lived alone in Arizona to watch William and Harry's weddings and all the preceding festivities live on television.

She'd never even told Sophia that particular fact, afraid her friend would have teased her mercilessly for her romantic sentiments. But, really, it was more than that. One of her first memories was watching Princess Diana's wedding while snuggled up with her mom in the early hours of the morning.

Either way, the time passed with Oliver in the car on the way to London had been entirely too pleasant for Joy's good.

They closed their doors and climbed into the car. Oliver started the ignition and glanced over at her. "Where to now?"

"What do you mean? We need to get this back to Soph." Heat poured from the SUV's vents, and Joy lifted her hands to warm them.

"You can't tell me you came all the way to London and aren't going to see a few sites. That just isn't right."

"Believe me, I'd love to. Do you know how many movies set in England I've seen? How often I've wanted to visit?" She still couldn't believe she was here. The skies were drearier than in her favorite films, and evidence of previous snowfall decorated the gutters. Even so, icy streets and storefronts strung with lights added a certain holiday spirit, enough to bring the magic of being here to life. "But we've got to get back. Sophia needs my help with a ton of stuff."

"I refuse to allow you to come to my city and not take in at least one place of notoriety."

The man was stubborn but so was she. "What

about the snow headed this way? Sophia said there was a good chance of it."

Oliver whipped out his phone and messed with it for a moment. "Ah. Looks to be several hours out. We'll be gone before then." Replacing it on his center console, he looked her square in the eyes. "So, what's it to be?"

Joy huffed, smiling to show him he'd won—and that she didn't hold a grudge. "Why don't you pick?

"I know just the place."

Half an hour later, he'd parked and walked them into Westminster Abbey. Joy took in the Gothic style of the centuries-old church where British coronations and some royal weddings were held. "This is a dream." She glanced at Oliver, who'd shoved his hands inside the pockets of his gray trench coat.

"You said you loved the monarchy and that you watched the Duke and Duchess of Cambridge's wedding, so . . ." He shrugged.

"It's perfect." She reached out and squeezed his arm. "Thank you for bringing me here."

They ventured inside and purchased tickets to a guided tour. Their verger—a caretaker of sorts who acted as a tour guide through the church—was an older man with a thinning pad of hair up top and a long black robe. He led them throughout the abbey, from Poets' Corner to the royal tombs and every other notable location within. Joy's fingers itched to take photos, but the abbey's policy didn't allow it.

Part of her was glad because it meant she could simply observe, pray, and enjoy her surroundings.

At the far eastern end of the church, the verger walked through large brass gates into what he called the Lady Chapel, or Henry VII's chapel. His spectacles caught the light flickering through the gorgeous high stained-glass windows as he described the late medieval architecture, evident in the fan-vaulted ceiling, where curving wood was carved equidistantly, creating the effect of ladies' fans spreading across the ornate ceiling.

Joy's neck hurt from straining to make out the designs on the dozens of banners hanging from above. According to the verger, these banners represented the Knights of the Order of Bath, and the nearly one hundred statues of saints interspersed between them displayed the largest surviving figure sculpture collection from Tudor England. Beneath the banners on either side of the main aisle, rows of mahogany stalls contrasted with the light-colored walls and ceiling.

"This is the resting place of fifteen monarchs, including Mary the First, Elizabeth the First, and Mary, Queen of Scots." The verger walked around the cavernous chapel with his hands behind his back.

Now that he mentioned it, she saw tombs scattered about the room. On the east side of the space rose two large gilt bronze effigies of Henry VII and his wife. The marble effigy of Elizabeth the First depicted a somber woman lying in her regal finery across the top of the tomb.

The soaring ceiling, the elegant details, the way the light swooped through the entire chapel—it all brought a beauty she couldn't describe, embedding it down deeply in her soul. This place that memorialized the dead was so gorgeous in its rendering, and it made Joy feel . . . alive.

How ironic.

Oliver leaned toward her. "Amazing, isn't it?" His whispered words brushed against the top of her ears.

"Hmm . . ."

"That's all you have to say?"

Her eyes found his, but although she saw teasing glinting beneath his lashes, she couldn't joke in this moment—not when, for the first time in a long time, she didn't feel so burdened. So frightened of what was to come. This monument to the Creator, meant to honor life even in death, gave her something physical yet other-worldly to cling to.

So yes, words wouldn't come. Joy could only express her gratitude to him for bringing her here by reaching out her hand and lacing her fingers between his.

Surprise lit his face but he didn't pull away. In fact, his hand grasped hers with a firmness that said he wasn't going to let go.

And something about this place and whatever

was happening inside of her . . . well, she was okay with that.

Her gaze left his and traveled upward, finding the light once more. And when she closed her eyes in reverence, it continued to shine even then.

THE TRIP to Westminster had taken much longer than she'd expected, and she wasn't the only one who had lost track of time.

As they made their way to the front of the abbey, Oliver checked his Orient dress watch. "Oh, wow. It's already half past three. How did that happen?"

"It was just so mesmerizing." And she didn't just mean the church, though it was deserving of that adjective. After their tour had ended, they'd wandered hand in hand, room to room, taking in the sights. Despite her usual affinity for talking, she found herself bound in a spell that she feared would break if they spoke, a spell she didn't want to emerge from until absolutely necessary.

Necessary had finally arrived.

Joy dropped Oliver's hand and dug in her purse for her phone. "How's the weather?" Her weather app should tell them, though it was never too reliable. She powered up her phone as they rounded the last corner toward the massive entrance. Other visitors exited and a blast of icy air hit Joy when she got close.

She dropped her phone into her bag. No weather app needed.

Snow fell from the gray sky at an alarming rate.

Joy turned to Oliver, whose brow furrowed. "You okay to drive in this?"

"I'm fine driving in snow, though this looks a mite heavy." Oliver buttoned his jacket and reached for her hand once more. "Come on. Let's get to the car, and I'll check the weather reports just to be sure."

She nestled her hand in his and ducked against the wind. By the time they reached his car, her head was wet from the falling flakes of white, her fingers stiff from the cold.

Oliver cranked the car heater and defroster, using his wipers to rid the windshield of the precipitation already gathering on the glass. "Wait just a moment while I take a look." He pulled his phone from his pocket, and his thumb danced across the screen.

Joy took the opportunity to text Sophia and let her know they'd been waylaid a bit but that she'd report in when they left.

A text came back immediately.

I'VE BEEN TRYING TO CALL YOU. IT'S ONLY SNOWING A LITTLE HERE, BUT BETWEEN PORT WILLIS AND LONDON, THE STORM LOOKS PRETTY FIERCE. IT'S

WAY MORE INTENSE THAN THEY THOUGHT. YOU
SHOULD STAY THERE UNTIL IT CLEARS.

Joy's fingers flew as she typed a reply.

BUT WE HAVE YOUR DRESS. AND YOU NEED MY
HELP.

Moments later, her phone dinged in response.

YOUR SAFETY IS WAY MORE IMPORTANT THAN ANY
DRESS. STAY PUT FOR TONIGHT. YOU CAN COME
TOMORROW ONCE THE ROADS ARE PLOWED AND IT'S
SAFE.

A groan escaped Joy's throat. "Sophia said she's
seen bad reports—"

"I think we should stay in town tonight," Oliver
said at the same time.

This was not the plan. But some things couldn't
be helped. "I just can't believe the weather stations
didn't warn us how bad it would be."

Through the windshield, Oliver peeked at the
sky. "I'm not sure how great American forecasters
are, but here they get it wrong all the time."

"Good point."

"So we're agreed then? We shouldn't venture
back to Cornwall today?"

"Yeah, I think so."

He put the car into DRIVE and eased onto the
road, which was already crammed with cars. To
their left and up the street a bit, a double-decker
tour bus driver honked.

"So where are we going?" There must be a dozen

hotels within walking distance, but based on the rate of snow coming down, they didn't have long to find shelter.

When he didn't answer, she glanced over. His face was a mask. "Oliver?"

He cleared his throat. "How would you feel about going to my place?" After a brief pause, he hurried on. "You can take my room, and I'll take the sofa, of course."

Unease rippled through Joy's stomach. But why? It was a practical solution, and she certainly didn't fear being alone with him.

Oh, please. She knew why and Joy couldn't lie to herself. Being with him in the car was one thing. Seeing his home, being among his things, sleeping in his bed—innocent though it might be—would only get her closer to stepping over the friendship line that stood between them. And once they'd crossed it, she knew there would be no going back.

Not with him.

But staying at his place was the best choice they had, right?

She forced a smile. "Sure. Sounds great."

CHAPTER 10

When they reached the tall black door of apartment 404, Joy held Sophia's dress while Oliver inserted a key into the lock. Opening the door, he flicked on the lights, took the garment bag from her, and invited her in.

Attempting to conceal the deep breath she inhaled, Joy stepped into Oliver's flat, the scent of something sweet greeting her. "Did you bake before you left?"

He kicked the front door closed and deposited the garment bag into a hall closet. "It's a candle my mum gave me. Warm biscuits or some such thing. It seems to give off a scent even when it's not lit."

They both removed their damp coats and hung them. Joy's sweater was blessedly dry, and her jeans were mostly so. They wouldn't be the most comfortable clothing to sleep in, but she'd make do.

The entryway connected to a hallway that opened on one side into a great room and kitchen with gorgeous stainless-steel appliances and a white marble countertop with swirls of gray. Joy's boots clipped along the real-wood plank flooring, a rich chestnut brown that shimmered as if it'd just been polished. From the open-concept kitchen, she could see a four-person wood table and chairs set in front of a floor-to-ceiling window granting a full view of Hyde Park, which was quickly becoming whiter by the moment.

How different his flat was from her former house in Arizona—all vintage and bright. But though it screamed designer, his home also gave off cozy vibes.

"Your place is lovely." Joy slipped off her shoes, not wanting to ruin the gorgeous Persian rug as she stepped up to the window to study what lay beyond. Her fingertips grazed the glass as she watched the lowering sun slip behind the clouds and snow swirl in the light of lamps that had turned on only moments before.

"Thank you." Now he stood beside her. "Make yourself comfortable. Please. My home is your home."

She pressed a hand to her chest. He had no idea how those words affected her.

Because she didn't have a home anymore. Not one of her own, anyway.

She shook herself from the melancholy thought. "I will. Thanks." Treading from the rug back onto the wood floors, she found her way to the leather tan wraparound couch that sat opposite a white brick fireplace flanked by elegant white bookcases. Before she sat, she flipped a switch on the wall and artificial flames leapt to life.

While Oliver rummaged in the kitchen for something to eat, Joy casually studied the rest of the living room. A home was often a good way to get to know people. It took her a moment to realize that he had no Christmas decor of any kind. Hmm. A dog bed lay in one corner, so out of place in the refined bachelor pad that she had to smile. She bet Rascal—whom Oliver had left behind with his aunt—was allowed on the couch, however much money it had cost.

On the mantle sat several framed photos. One displayed Oliver with his parents, younger brother, and a woman in a bridal gown—his sister-in-law, she'd guess. Another showed him hugging two young girls to him, his smile easy. In the last one, Oliver stood with his arm around a beautiful woman whose black dress showed off her long, tan legs.

A twinge of something Joy didn't want to address sliced through her.

She turned her attention from the pictures to a thick book beside them. Joy approached but had to rise on her tiptoes to make out the book's title. *The*

Holy Bible on the spine gleamed back at her in silvery letters.

"How do water biscuits, cheese, and ham sound for dinner?"

She turned to find him with a tray. "Water biscuits?" Glancing at the food selection, she laughed. "Oh, crackers."

Oliver grinned. "Crackers, sure. Do you want to head to the table?"

The warmth of the fire was so inviting, the rolling flames so soothing. "Would you mind if we ate over here?"

"Not at all." He glanced at the couch but lowered himself to the ground in front of it, which was covered by a silk rug. Setting the tray down, he patted the spot next to him. "Join me?"

"Of course." Joy sat on the soft rug and snagged a cracker from the platter, placing a thick slice of Gouda on top. "*Bon appétit.*" She lifted the cracker as if in a toast.

Oliver quickly grabbed a cracker of his own and hit it softly against hers. "I'm sorry it's not more of a feast."

"Are you kidding? It's perfect. Pretty much how I eat at home, especially when it's just me. And that's fairly often since Mom went into the rehab facility."

"How is she?"

Joy thought back to the call she'd made to her parents before she and Oliver had entered Westminster Abbey. "Pretty good, all things considered. She's making progress with the physical therapy, and they think she could be home by just after New Year's."

"I'm sure that's a relief to hear."

"Yeah, it is."

A silence fell between them as they ate and watched the fire. Oliver turned on the radio, and soft Christmas music lilted through the room.

Joy used her napkin to wipe her mouth. "I noticed you don't have any Christmas decor."

"It's just me and Rascal here, and I knew I'd be gone for the actual holiday." He took the empty platter from between them and placed it on a side table next to the couch. "It seemed a waste to spend time decorating when I'm the only one who would see it."

Considering his words, she stared into the fire. Whether intentional or not, the orange flames in the fireplace provided the only light in the room, creating a soft glow that didn't reach the shadowed corners. The halo effect surrounded them, limiting the outside world.

"I don't think beauty is ever a waste. And to me, there's nothing better than sitting in front of a Christmas tree as its lights sparkle, thinking about the magic of the season, the fact that love came down to us when we least deserved it."

"I see your point. And maybe I can't think of

anything better." He paused. "But I can think of something that's just as good."

She felt the heat of his gaze on her. When she swiveled to look at him, his eyes drank her in.

They'd ended up close together, the sides of her right leg and arm just brushing against his. The air pulsed with emotion.

Get up. Leave. Say goodnight. Nothing lasting can come from this.

Joy should listen to her inner self. But instead, she spoke, the words nearly strangling her. "And what's that?"

Slowly, methodically, Oliver twisted to face her more directly and lifted his hand to her face. His thumb trailed her cheekbone upward. "It's good to be sitting here, with you, listening to holiday music, eating a pathetic excuse for a dinner. I'm loving every moment of it."

"Hey, the food wasn't that bad."

He smiled. "And there you go joking, but I'm serious. Joy, I've never met anyone like you before, with such a zest for life and such a heart for others. I feel more alive just being near you. And to be quite honest . . . I'm mad about you."

She couldn't force her eyes off him, couldn't speak. All her objections and questions swirled away with the snow that fell outside.

He saw her. He understood her. He . . . wanted her.

And she wanted him.

It might not be a winning scenario, but right now, she almost didn't care. Kicking the last shred of doubt to the momentary curb, she allowed herself to speak the truth. "I feel the same way."

With a smile, he moved his face nearer, and before she could close her eyes, his lips skimmed hers.

And then, the fire died.

JOY JOLTED AWAKE.

Despite the socks on her feet and the pile of blankets Oliver had loaned her, she shivered.

What time was it? The darkness outside the curtains indicated it was still the middle of the night. Had she slept long? If so, it didn't feel like it. Maybe that's because subconsciously she'd spent the time lying on Oliver's pillow smelling the remnants of his extremely manly shampoo and thinking about the kiss that had only lasted a second.

Joy pulled the comforter tighter around her. If only they hadn't been interrupted by the power going out last night. It had certainly broken the magic of the moment. When they'd been plunged into darkness, Oliver managed to locate two flashlights and call the power company using his cell phone. The storm was to blame, of course, so who knew when power would be restored.

Maybe the interruption had been for the best.

She tried rolling over and going back to sleep, but her brain and her freezing body wouldn't let her. Maybe moving would help. Or eating. That was supposed to warm you up, right? Worth a shot. She didn't want to wake Oliver, who had bunked in the living room, but maybe she could quietly scrounge for something in the kitchen.

Rising from the bed, she pulled one of the thick quilts around her shoulders, grabbed the flashlight, and clicked it on to its lowest brightness. As she opened the door to Oliver's bedroom, a squeak resounded from the hinges. She winced and continued, passing his office on the way. When she reached the kitchen, she glanced over at the couch where Oliver was supposed to be sleeping.

"Couldn't sleep either?"

Joy whirled, dropped her blanket, and shone her light toward the eat-in-nook. Her gaze landed upon Oliver shading his eyes with his hand. Joy quickly clicked off the flashlight and waited for her eyes to adjust to the dimness.

He sat bundled in one of his kitchen chairs, which was turned toward the window. Everything remained dark out there except for a small sliver of moonlight somehow breaking through the clouds. It appeared as if someone was tossing white confetti from the sky. The snow fell at all angles: straight downward, diagonally, some nearly perpendicular to the ground she couldn't see but knew was there.

And other than Oliver's question, the room was devoid of sound.

The fact the storm had not abated did cause her some temporary distress—what would happen if they couldn't make it back to Cornwall soon?—but the tranquility of the moment was too great to allow such a thought to ruin it.

In reply, Joy simply pushed her feet forward and pulled up a chair next to Oliver.

He opened his blanket and wrapped it and his arm around her shoulders, insulating her in his warmth.

She laid her head in the crook of his arm.

"Happy Christmas Eve." He whispered the words against her hair, sending a shiver down her spine.

"It's past midnight?"

"According to my battery-operated wall clock, yes."

She attempted to adjust the blanket, and her hand bumped against his. Feeling brave, she wove their palms and fingers together. "Where were you this time last year?"

"Probably in bed."

Her laughter spilled into the silence. "Okay, not sometime between midnight and morning, but Christmas Eve. Mom and I decorated cookies. My parents and I attended the candlelight service at church, grabbed some delicious takeout for dinner, and ended the night by watching *White Christmas*. The perfect day." Her lips arced upward at the happy memory. "Christmas Day was another story. Mom had a meltdown and so did I. But Christmas Eve . . . that was one for the books."

"I'm glad for that." His thumb stroked the top of hers and he sighed. "As for me, I spent the day with family. But it was supposed to be my wedding day."

She straightened and pulled away to face him. The blanket keeping them wrapped together drooped. "Supposed to be?"

He took a moment to finish his thought. His fingers pressed against her hand as if wanting to anchor it there. The clouds broke a bit, allowing more starlight through. Joy could make out the contours of Oliver's face, his mouth falling into a frown. "My fiancée ended things a year ago in October."

"I'm sorry. What happened, if you don't mind me asking?"

"I don't mind. That's why I'm telling you." He shifted. Was he itching to pull her close again like she hoped he would? But she needed to focus on his words, not on how wonderful it felt to be enveloped in his embrace.

"Jana and I dated for three years before I finally worked up the nerve to propose. We were extremely busy people—she an interior decorator and me a business owner. After I proposed, things were good for a while but business picked up. A lot. So I dedicated more hours to growing it, maybe partially because I wanted to be successful when my previous venture had failed but also because so many employees depended on me. I went from five to twenty in a span of a few months. Those people had spouses, children, elderly parents to care for. The pressure was intense."

"That's understandable." She squeezed his hand in a show of support.

"Even so, I lost Jana because of it. She got tired of me showing up late and canceling on her for dates, wedding planning appointments, you name it. I even stopped going to church because I could squeeze in a few extra hours of work if I did. I had the right motivation but the wrong priorities."

"You were putting others first. That can't be wrong."

"It was if I started to see myself as some kind of savior. And I did. I thought it was solely on my shoulders to save my employees from ruin the way I'd been ruined years before that. But it wasn't. Because I forgot to factor in one thing." He paused. "I forgot to factor in God."

Something jabbed her spirit, and she turned her eyes back to the snow—the thing that was keeping her from "saving" Sophia. "I think I can relate to that sentiment."

"Maybe we're two peas in a pod after all then, eh?"

That got a laugh. "Maybe so." A sudden thought came to her, unbidden. Joy bit her lip. "Is Jana the woman in the photo on the mantle?" The one who made the Oliver beside her look so happy?

"Yes."

"So . . ." How did she ask the question on her mind without coming across as insecure and . . . well . . . petty?

"So does that mean I'm not over her?"

"I guess so. Yeah."

"I'm not going to lie. When she ended our engagement, it nearly broke me. There were several mornings that the only thing that got me out of bed was that my employees depended on me. But then, the Lord woke me up, reminded me that the sun keeps on rising and setting, that his mercies are new every morning."

"That's a great revelation . . . but why keep her photo on the mantle where you're going to continue seeing it? Why subject yourself to that pain?"

"I suppose it's a reminder. That sometimes, the things God has planned for our lives aren't what we expect. But they're good. Somehow, they're good." Oliver lifted their connected hands, pulling them from underneath the blanket. He brought his lips to the top of her hand, kissing it with all the tenderness of an English gentleman in one of her favorite films. Then, his eyes found hers. "And I didn't expect you, Joy Beckman."

The breath whooshed from her. This was it. The moment of no return—the moment her heart would start its descent toward, eventually, fully breaking.

But with the snow coming down just outside, the promise of a new day on the horizon, and the beautiful words he'd just spoken, Joy couldn't do anything but fall.

With her free hand, she stroked his disarray of hair, pushing her fingers through it, then curving them down around the back of his head, her thumb grazing his ear. She scooted sideways in her chair toward him and lifted her face, inviting him into her sphere.

He dropped her hand and cupped her chin, staring at her through the darkness, the intensity in his gaze not lost on her despite the lack of light. And then he leaned forward and brushed his lips against hers once, twice, three times before he deepened the kiss.

Joy looped her other arm around his neck, pulling him to her. And in that moment, they became like two falling snowflakes that were drawn to each other—impossible to separate.

CHAPTER 11

"This is quite possibly the best egg casserole I've ever tasted in my life." Joy almost moaned as she placed the last bite of Ginny's Christmas morning dish into her mouth, chewing, relishing the way the sausage mingled with the egg.

"It's a really simple recipe," Ginny said from her spot on the carpeted floor next to Sophia's Christmas tree.

"You say that, but I'm sure I'd find a way to screw it up." Sophia set her fork onto her empty plate and plopped back against her couch cushions. "Joy is right. That was amazing. I know you specialize in baked goods, but you really should just open a restaurant."

Ginny pulled her legs into her chest and wrapped her arms around her knees. "I already have a bazillion items I want to add to my bakery menu. An entire restaurant would make it impossible to narrow down."

Outside, as the sun proclaimed it a cloudless day, the sky had already forgotten the storm that had nearly caused Joy and Oliver to miss Christmas in Port Willis. But, the snow had stopped the previous morning—though it was due to start again today in London and Cornwall—and by afternoon, the plows had done their thing. Whatever the reason, Joy had felt a strange mixture of gratitude to be heading back to Sophia and sadness over the beginning of the end as it concerned her relationship with Oliver.

If cuddling and kissing a bunch and talking about anything and everything for less than a day constituted a relationship.

Joy sipped the hot apple cider Ginny had simmered on the stovetop early this morning. The toasty liquid warmed her lips and throat as she snuggled under a blanket, her eyes roaming Sophia's beautifully decorated tree and landing on the framed painting of a couple cradling a baby thousands of years ago—a baby who would become King.

The steam from her mug filled her lungs. Between whatever she had going on with Oliver and her mom's deteriorating health, Joy had much to worry about. But today was a day for thankfulness. A day to remember that hope would always trump the things that troubled her.

"So how about we open a few gifts before the guys get here?" Sophia stood and knelt beside the tree, sorting through the gifts until she located a large bag and a medium-sized box with a glittery gold bow.

William, Steven, and Oliver were joining them for Christmas lunch before the latter two joined their families for dinner. Joy was nearly giddy at the thought of seeing her man again.

My man. Oh, brother. Slow your roll, Joy.

"You guys, I feel like the worst friend in the world. I didn't have a chance to go shopping yet." Ginny ran her fingers under her eyes. "I haven't purchased a single item for anyone . . . not even Steven."

"Girl, don't sweat it. We know you've been busy." Sophia handed her the gift bag and set the box on the oak coffee table in front of Joy. "And I have a feeling Steven doesn't need some store-bought gift to make him the happiest man in the world on Christmas."

Curling her fingers around her mug, Joy leaned forward in her seat. "Did I miss something?" With all the commotion over retrieving the dress and getting stuck in London, she'd forgotten to ask Ginny how things had gone with Steven.

Ginny's cheeks turned a delightful shade of pink. "He and I had a nice chat the other night."

"Uh, details?"

"Sophia's already heard it all. I'd hate to bore her—"

"As if you could." With a happy sigh, Sophia sank back onto the couch and hugged a red, fringed pillow. "I mean, I never get tired of watching *You've Got Mail*, so why would hearing about my friend's romantic exploits be any different?"

"Oh, this sounds good." And if the attention were on Ginny, it wouldn't be on Joy and *her* romantic exploits—the details of which she had yet to divulge to either woman. To anyone, actually. She'd been too exhausted when she'd slipped in late last night. "You've definitely got to dish now."

Light spilled from Ginny's smile. She tucked a strand of hair behind her ear. "After I left here on Sunday, I had lunch with Steven and his parents, as you know. We've met several times before, and they're lovely people."

"The loveliest. Now, skip to the really good part."

Ginny stuck her tongue out at Sophia. "Ha ha. Fine." She turned her attention back to Joy. "For dinner, I thought we'd go to this eclectic diner we like to visit every time I'm in town. But instead, he took me to his houseboat, where he made spaghetti."

"Ah, a man who can cook. I like it." *Does Oliver cook?* Joy pushed away the thought because a detail like that didn't matter. She probably wouldn't be involved with him long enough to find out.

"Well, he tried, anyway. Let's just say it was

adorable." Ginny bit her lip, smiling at the memory. "After we ate, we moved to his couch and chatted about our plans for Christmas, a little about the wedding, and about my plans for the bakery. Basically, everything but what we really needed to talk about. Finally, I got up my courage and told him how I felt."

"What does that mean? What did you say?" Joy usually allowed others to tell a story without interruption but couldn't seem to contain her questions today.

Ginny's fingers rustled against the red tissue paper sticking out from her gift bag. "Kind of what I said to you guys the other day. I told him I wanted to move back and open a bakery here, but I was afraid it was for the wrong reasons. He asked what I meant, and I said, 'I'm afraid I want to do it because you're here.'" She paused, a tear sliding down her cheek. "Then he turned to me and said, 'Ginny, open the bakery wherever you want. Don't you know that I'd move to London, Paris—even back to Boston, if that's where you wanted to go?" She paused. "Which I don't, by the way. Even though part of me would love to show my parents how successful I'm going to be. But I digress. He basically said if I wasn't going to open a bakery here, he'd uproot his life and go wherever I was. The only reason he hasn't done it yet was to give me time to decide what I wanted to do. Time to heal from Garrett's betrayal and the divorce. Time to find God and become secure in my knowledge of who I really am."

Now Sophia and Joy both had tears in their eyes too.

Joy's tears originated from happiness for Ginny and Steven. But she recognized another source as well. An ache had formed in the pit of her heart, and it had everything to do with how she'd perhaps finally found such a man for herself but eventually would have to let him go. How could he possibly fit into her life?

She'd considered it at all angles. If things ever came to the point where they fell in love, fully and completely, how would they be together? Joy's parents needed her, so there was no way she could move half a world away. And Oliver's employees and the success of his company meant everything to him. She wouldn't be the woman who took him away from that.

"And that right there is the sign of a good man." Sophia nearly bounced in her seat. "Tell her the rest."

"Yes, please." Joy steadied her voice. "And don't leave anything out."

"All right, all right." Ginny laughed, wiping away her tears. "What he said stunned me, frankly. And it made me realize that even though I initially came to Port Willis for a man—Garrett—it's still home. The people I love the most in the world are here. And yeah, I could bake anywhere, but I want to bake here.

It was just fear keeping me from admitting that before. So I have a meeting scheduled tomorrow about renting the space next to the bookstore. And Soph and I have already started talking about opening a wall between the two so customers can flow between our stores. We'll have to talk to the city about it and get the permits and everything, but . . . yeah. It's super exciting."

"That's fabulous, Ginny. I'm so happy for you."

"Yes, super-duper exciting." Sophia looked pointedly at Ginny. "But if you don't tell her what happened with Steven, I'm gonna do it for you."

Joy nudged her best friend. "Man, when did you get so bossy?"

"Been hanging around you too much, I guess."

Joy and Sophia laughed then returned their attention to Ginny.

"After he told me that, he took my hands in his, looked me straight in the eyes, and said, 'Ginny Rose, you've done amazing things over the past year. Simply amazing. And even though you said you didn't know who you were, I did. And I love that woman. I love you.'"

Joy and Sophia sighed at the declaration.

Now Ginny was full-on happy crying. "I know, right? How did I get so lucky? So then I blubbered and blabbered on, I don't really know about what— you know me—but eventually I said I loved him too."

Joy's fingers drummed against the gift on her lap.

"That's pretty much the best story ever." *Will I ever have one like it?*

She'd never asked that before, not for years, anyway. When Sophia and William had gotten together last year, she'd felt nothing but joy for them. Nothing. Not one iota of comparison or jealousy or anything.

Now, though?

She wished she could pause time so this week would last forever.

No. She knew her future, and she'd always been okay with it. One romantic holiday with a guy she barely knew wouldn't change that. If she could just stay focused on how this was temporary and try to enjoy herself anyway, then maybe it would be a nice story to keep for herself if she ever gave loneliness an inch in her life.

"Yes, it is. Now." Sophia swung her gaze toward Joy. "Don't think you're getting out of telling us about what happened in London." Her eyebrows rose and her lips quirked.

At that moment, the doorbell chimed. The guys had arrived.

Joy released a sigh—saved by the bell, literally— and hopped up. "That will have to wait, I guess."

No, she couldn't put off Sophia forever, but for now, her heart raced in anticipation of spending time with Oliver again. *Merry Christmas to me.*

How was this her life? Joy felt as if she'd walked onto the set of a Christmas movie.

A gentle snow fell where she stood just outside Sophia's house, caressing her cheeks and eyelashes. It had been fluttering down since lunch time, so a few inches covered the ground. According to Sophia, the dusting would melt rather quickly once it warmed up, which was supposed to happen tomorrow—just in time for the wedding in three days.

Oliver stood beside her, one arm looped around her shoulders, Rascal at his feet. Together, they watched the slow fluff twirl to meet the sleepy town. The street remained quiet, not a car or person about. Chimneys puffed out curls of smoke, and the lamp-post she'd begun to think of as "theirs" emitted a soft glow.

Once again, it was just the two of them in a world of subtle color and peace.

"What are you thinking?" Oliver's breath warmed her ear.

Joy pulled her gaze from the sky and connected it with his. "That this has been such a lovely day." Feeling bold, she snagged his free hand. She'd have tugged him to sit on the bench next to the lamp, but snow covered the wooden slats. "And that this is the perfect way to end Christmas Day."

He leaned down to give her a kiss—too quick but still potent. They'd managed to sneak a few pecks here and there, but with so many of their friends crowding into Sophia's tiny house to celebrate the holiday, there hadn't been much occasion to be alone until now. "And it's not quite over yet."

"What do you mean?"

He lowered his arm and opened his thick gray coat. From the inside pocket, he plucked something flat wrapped in tissue paper. "It isn't much, but I thought you may fancy them."

Joy carefully took Oliver's gift in her purple-mittened hand. The paper crinkled as she unfolded it from what felt like cardstock of some sort. As soon as she saw the picture of two large mice, Joy couldn't help the laugh that fell from her lips. She flipped through the same vintage Christmas cards she'd been eyeing in the antique shop the first day they'd met—ten in all—each one more ridiculous than the last.

"Thank you." Biting her lip, she glanced at him again. "But I didn't get you anything."

"I'm sure you can think of something." Humor glinted in his eye.

"Hmm." As Joy slipped the cards inside her jacket, she turned to face him. "How about a nice pat on the back?"

"That'd be great—if I were Rascal."

"A hug, then?"

Oliver stepped closer and put his hands around her waist. "Getting warmer."

"Yes, a hug *would* make me warmer, thanks." Despite the chill of the snow against her face, her lips twisted into a full-on grin. This was too fun.

He pulled her to him, and she snuggled against his chest. How did she fit so perfectly here in a place she hadn't known existed more than a week ago?

After a few moments of delicious heat, she glanced up and quirked an eyebrow. "I do have one more idea . . ."

"And what's that?"

"A kiss, of course."

"I suppose I could accept that."

"You have to come closer, though. A girl can only lift on her tiptoes so much."

He complied and their noses nearly touched.

Joy's arms encircled his neck as she grazed her lips against his cheek. "There you go. Merry Christmas."

His chuckle shot joy right into her heart. "That's probably the best gift I'll receive this year or any other."

And somehow, she believed he meant it. "Challenge accepted."

"What challenge is that?"

Looking at him with mock sincerity, Joy blinked rapidly. "The challenge of giving you an even better gift every year, of course."

Something shifted in his eyes, from joking to serious in two seconds flat. Then she realized what she'd said. How she'd sounded. What she'd presumed. Joy swallowed hard. She hadn't meant to . . .

But trying to explain away that she'd made some giant implications would only be awkward, so she did what she'd been longing to do all day.

She snagged his lips with her own.

His arms tightened around her back, and her arms dragged him closer so there wasn't much between them other than her questions. But with every moment locked in his embrace, Joy steadily released her doubts. A continual ebb and flow of deepening and lightening kisses continued as the passion mounted inside her, an aching need pulsing, begging to escape. She felt it all the way to the toes curled inside her pink boots.

Finally, she broke away, needing to catch her breath. Her head spun and her pulse galloped as Oliver crushed her to his chest. The rapid beating of his heart proved she wasn't the only one affected by their chemistry.

"I very much look forward to seeing how you top that in future." His whisper sent a thrill of longing and sorrow through her.

What future?

Maybe she could banish the thought if she lingered here, anchored in the beauty of the present. Joy closed her eyes and inhaled the scent of him.

Oliver's fingers played with a short strand of her hair as he continued holding her. "I need to go but I don't want to." Dinner with his aunt and a few of her friends was supposed to begin at six, and it had already been five forty-five when they'd come outside.

"And I need to go inside." Sophia's mom would arrive in the morning, and Ginny had headed off to spend the evening with Steven's family, so tonight it'd just be her, Sophia, and William. "But I don't want to either."

"I suppose I'll be the responsible one then." Icy cold met Joy's cheeks upon his release. The twinkling lights strung along Sophia's roof illuminated his teasing smile. "Will I see you tomorrow?"

"I hope so. Thank you again for the cards. I love them."

"You're welcome. And I think it will come as no surprise that I loved your gift as well—and the enthusiasm with which you gave it."

Surely she'd left him in no doubt of her feelings. "Merry Christmas, Oliver."

"Merry Christmas, Joy."

With that, she spun on her heel and hightailed it inside the house, leaning against the door after she'd shut it.

"Well, well, well. Looking a bit flushed, are we?"

Sophia stood in front of her, arms crossed, a huge grin plastered on her face.

Joy peeled off her mittens and parka, which she hung on the coatrack before moving into the living room. "It was cold outside. Where's William?"

"He said he's taking a nap in my room, but I think he just wanted to give us a chance to catch up. And don't change the subject." Sophia followed her into the room and plopped onto the couch. On her television, she'd queued up a Christmas station that featured a roaring fire and played holiday tunes at a low volume.

In the bleak midwinter, frosty wind made moan. Earth stood hard as iron, water like a stone . . .

"Who, me?" Joy couldn't bring herself to sit just yet, so she wandered to the front window next to the Christmas tree. Peeking through the curtains, she could just make out Oliver and Rascal's retreating forms.

Snow had fallen, snow on snow, snow on snow. In the bleak midwinter, long ago.

"You really like him, huh?" Sophia's voice had dropped all teasing.

Joy turned to face her best friend again. "Yeah."

"I haven't seen you this gone over a guy since . . . well, never, actually. There was Chase, but even he only lasted three dates."

"I know, Soph, but there's no future between me and Oliver thanks to the small matter of my parents and his job. It's just not realistic." But oh, how right it had felt being in his arms. That had been real enough.

In the bleak midwinter, a stable-place sufficed. The Lord God Almighty—Jesus Christ.

"That's what I thought when I first started to fall for William. I didn't think it would work out. But look at us now." Sophia patted the spot next to her on the couch.

Dragging her feet, Joy walked over and slumped against the cushions. She snatched a pillow and hugged it to her chest, focusing her gaze on the undulating flames flickering on the TV. "It's different for you. You didn't have anything tying you down in the States." Joy cringed. "I don't mean it like that. I love my parents."

"Of course you do." Sophia snuggled close to Joy, each woman supporting the other—a symbol for their friendship if ever there were one. "Did you consider what I said last week about applying for some jobs?"

"Yes. I subscribed to a site with job postings." She thought about the notifications she'd received already for therapist jobs in her area. None of them had been quite what she'd be looking for, but Joy had to admit a flicker of longing at the thought of returning to counseling women who needed help.

"That's a great step."

"Thanks for encouraging me to do it. All of this

with Mom and Dad, the move to Florida, selling my practice . . . it's just been an overwhelming time."

"I'm sorry I haven't been there with you. And to throw a wrench in things with my wedding."

"Stop it." Joy nudged her with an elbow. "There's nowhere I'd rather be."

"I'm guessing part of that has nothing to do with me."

Joy groaned. Her friend wasn't going to let up with the Oliver stuff, was she? "You got me. Obviously, I'm enjoying the scenery too."

"I'll bet you are."

They laughed and the fire on the television danced.

What can I give Him, poor as I am?

"Joy." Sophia's words came out soft, cautious. "Are you ever going to tell me what happened between you and Oliver in London?"

Yet what I can I give Him, give my heart.

"Of course. I'll tell you everything, friend."

CHAPTER 12

"Hey, Mom." Joy slipped from the warmth of the giant manor where Sophia's rehearsal lunch was in full swing.

Though it was a surprising fifty-two degrees and the recent snow had never reached the town of Wendall where the wedding venue was located—about fifty miles from Port Willis—the air still vibrated with a chill. She stepped into a gorgeous garden that wound from the house down toward a magnificent, ancient-looking tree that overlooked a bluff. Many plants in the garden lay dormant, but other flowers and trees of all colors and varieties decorated either side of a crushed gravel walkway.

Joy stared at a pink rhododendron bush as she tried to focus on her mom. "How are you feeling?"

"Oh, just fine, dear." The vague tone in her mother's voice indicated that she might not remember who she was talking to—despite that *she* had called Joy—but she was putting on a good show nonetheless. A wet cough rattled across the phone.

Joy straightened. "That didn't sound good."

"It's just this cold I've had. It's been bothering me for days."

"You have a cold?" She'd called her parents two days ago on Christmas, but Mom hadn't been up to talking, and Dad hadn't mentioned Mom was sick.

If Joy had been there, she'd have known. Instead, she'd spent the time helping Sophia with last-minute details and fitting in as much time with Oliver as possible. She should have tried calling them again before now.

"Are the nurses taking good care of you?" Joy stuck her free hand into her parka pocket.

"Of course, of course."

Another cough put Joy on high alert. "Mom, are you sure you're okay? Has Dr. Lieberman been to see you yet? He should check your lungs, make sure they're clear."

"Stuff and nonsense. I'll be right as rain after a few nights of rest."

"Can I talk to Dad, please?" She started walking in order to stay warm. As she rounded a bend in the garden path, the sun popped out of the shade and warmed Joy's cheeks.

"No, he . . . well, I don't remember where he went."

"That's okay, Mom. Don't worry about it." Joy breathed a sigh of frustration. In about three days, she'd be back in Florida, monitoring Mom's care more closely. She simply had to trust that her mother would be fine until then and that others were capable of caring for her in the interim.

Yeah, right. There was nothing *simple* about that.

After a few minutes of sharing the wedding plans for the next day, Joy came into view of the tree where Sophia and William's rehearsal had been held an hour ago. The wedding party had stood along the cliff, which offered a stunning prospect of the ocean but also wind that had pummeled them. Thank goodness for a blessedly brief ceremony and strategically placed outdoor heaters, or Joy would have frozen solid.

Now that same wind howled across the phone, making it difficult to hear Mom. "Sorry, what was that?"

"I'm tired."

"I'll let you go. Thanks for calling. Love you."

Mom hung up without saying another word. Even though Joy knew the disease was the reason Mom rarely acknowledged her love anymore, it felt like rejection and rejection always stung.

She stuck her phone into the back pocket of her jeans and leaned against the tree, watching the swirling depths of the ocean below. Her chaotic hair tickled the tips of her ears as it twirled with the gushes of air being sent upward.

"There you are." Oliver's comment nearly got lost on the crazy gale as he joined her at the tree. "The bride was looking for you. Apparently it's time for them to say a few thank-yous."

"All right." Joy couldn't keep the sadness from tingeing her words. With every moment that passed, normal life beckoned her back. Never had she been one to run away from her problems, but if she could only slow time . . .

"What's wrong, love?"

She bit her lip, tears nearly finding her eyes. "I just talked to my mom."

"Ah." His arm slipped around her shoulders, and she felt safe there, buffeted from the roiling draft coming up from the sea. Amazing how he understood her—that she didn't necessarily need to talk out the pain again. That she simply needed a companion to walk through it with her.

Oh, goodness. She really was going to full-on cry if she didn't get out of here and back to Sophia, so she put her arm around Oliver's waist and directed them toward the garden.

As they neared the house, Oliver stopped, holding Joy with him. He dropped his arm and framed her face with both hands, stroking her cheeks with his thumbs. "I'm sorry for your pain, Joy."

And that was all it took. Big plops of salty water streamed from her eyes onto his fingers. He took her into his arms and held her while she sobbed, soaking his brown cashmere sweater in the process.

After her tears died down, she pulled back slightly and looked up at him. "Thank you." Her nose felt nearly blocked and her makeup was sure to be in shambles. "You wouldn't happen to have a handkerchief, would you?"

"I'm not *that* old."

A smile flitted across her face at the tease. "But it would be British of you, wouldn't it?"

"I'm sorry to disappoint."

"Guess you can't believe everything you see in the movies." She knuckled away the excess moisture from under her eyes as she laughed.

"Real life can be better than the movies." He swooped in for a kiss that was over far too quickly. But the look in the depths of his brown eyes speared her. "This is madness, Joy."

"What?" Her words were soft as the petals of the Christmas roses blooming in the bush to their right.

"The way I feel about you."

She was afraid to ask what he meant by it.

He snatched her hand in his. "It came on like that winter snow the day we were in London. So quick, I'm not sure either of us saw it coming. And I don't know about you, but I've never experienced something this powerful before."

That certainly couldn't be true. "What about with Jana?"

"Jana and I were childhood chums, and things between us developed slowly. Looking back, I'm not sure I loved her in the right way, as a husband should love a wife. It was more like best mates who settled into a romance."

"My favorite romantic movie trope is friends-turned-lovers." Anne and Gilbert. Harry and Sally. Emma and Knightley. "I always imagined that's how my story would go."

You don't have a story. This is it. A chance encounter. A winter romance. Nothing more.

But she wanted it to be more.

For the first time, she allowed herself to dream. What would it be like to leave responsibility in the dust and pursue a relationship with Oliver after Sophia's wedding and beyond? To see it through?

Ugh, she was a horrible daughter to even consider it. Her parents had always been there for her when she needed them. How could she possibly do any less?

They began to saunter down the path arm in arm. Oliver's cologne wafted toward her, the scent fresh and deep. "What's going on in that brilliant mind of yours?"

"Just thinking."

"About . . ."

"The future."

The pressure of his arm around her increased slightly as he kissed the top of her head. "Don't borrow trouble."

Might as well say it. Break the bubble now. "What are we doing, Oliver? There's no future between us."

"You don't know that."

She gently disengaged herself from him. "I like you, Oliver. I really do. But that doesn't change the facts. And we're too old to play make believe." Her throat burned with the admission because that is just what she'd been doing—allowing herself to be swept away by the magic of the season, of Sophia's fairytale ending.

"I'm not pretending, Joy." Oliver moved toward her again, his boots crunching the gravel.

If only he'd stop looking at her like Charles Bingley looked at Jane Bennett, like Joe Fox looked at Kathleen Kelly, like Luke Danes looked at Lorelai Gilmore. "I'm not saying there's nothing between us. Clearly, there is. But it's just not realistic. There's nowhere for it to go. I'm not the kind of woman to pursue a relationship that's impossible before it begins. And you don't strike me as that kind of guy either."

"Why is it impossible? Simply because we live in different countries?"

"Don't you see that as a problem?"

"I admit it's not ideal, but it doesn't make things

impossible. Just more complicated. But Joy, you're worth *complicated*."

Why did he have to be so wonderful and smooth and . . . wonderful? Clearly, her brain was mush around him. She closed her eyes at the thought, focusing on the problem at hand. "I appreciate you saying that. But there's no way I can abandon my parents. They depend on me, and I won't let them down." Not again, anyway.

"And you have no idea how much I admire you for it."

Her eyes opened again, and she tilted her head. "Then you wouldn't ever ask me to do it. And unless you're willing to leave your business behind . . ."

His jaw clenched.

"Exactly." She softened her voice and squeezed his upper arm.

"You're not leaving room for another possibility."

Was there really something she hadn't considered? "And what's that?"

"That there's some other solution that neither of us can see right now because it's *not* the future. Only God knows what will happen, and he can work anything out."

"I know that God *can* work things out but he doesn't always." Case in point—instead of Mom and Dad living out their retirement traveling the world as they'd always intended, they were stuck in the clutches of Alzheimer's and a slow, agonizing separation thanks to the disease. "We have to make the best decisions we can with the information we have right now."

"Normally I would readily agree to using logic in decision making. But sometimes the heart can't be told how to feel." Behind him, a radiant display of yellow flowers adorned an evergreen shrub. "Joy, do you know the last time it snowed in Cornwall? It's been years. And do you know the last time it snowed here at Christmas time? Even longer. Yet, it happened. A year ago, we couldn't have predicted it. In fact, a year ago it was unusually warm at Christmastime. So, we can't tell the future, true. But you're forgetting one thing about the information we have right now."

"And what's that?" She couldn't keep the tremble from her voice.

"That what we're feeling for each other, it's rare. And it's a gift."

This was crazy. She'd always scoffed at the movies in which a couple met and fell hard for each other in a matter of days, yet that's what had happened.

Oliver looked at her with such longing that it stole her breath. All she wanted to do in the moment was burrow into his arms, forgetting that such things as Alzheimer's and oceans and responsibility even existed. But what good would it do? In a matter of days, she'd return to the United States. He'd return to London. And their time together would be nothing but a lovely and picturesque memory she'd hold onto when times got even tougher.

Joy swallowed, hard. "You're right. It's a beautiful gift. And I don't want to ruin the memory of it by arguing. It'd be easier to end it now instead of allowing things to grow bitter between us."

"Joy."

"I'm sorry, Oliver. I have to focus on Sophia right now. I'm supposed to be here for her, after all."

Then she rose up on her tiptoes, kissed his cheek, buried her hands into her jacket so she wouldn't reach for him again, and headed inside the manor.

CHAPTER 13

There couldn't be a more beautiful day for a more beautiful bride.

Joy's heart snagged at the sight of Sophia standing before a floor-length mirror in her A-line dress with beaded appliqués and capped sleeves. The basque waistline, tulle skirt with a lace hem, and chapel train worked together to perfectly highlight Sophia's allure. Her bright eyes and red lips popped even more than usual against the white of the dress. Tendrils of black curls framed her face, and her mouth pulled into a soft smile as she allowed her mom to hug her shoulders from behind.

She was Snow White about to marry her prince, and despite Joy's woes in the love department, she couldn't have been happier for her best friend.

"You are lovelier than any bride I've ever seen—

and I've seen a lot." Sandy Barrett's voice wobbled as she squeezed her daughter. Stepping away, she straightened the portrait neckline of her elegant silver gown. Not many women of sixty-one could pull off the asymmetrically ruched bodice, dropped waistline, and cascading ruffles, but Sandy wore it well.

Sophia batted away the beginning of a tear before it could fall. "I won't cry. I won't cry."

Joy flounced past fellow bridesmaids Ginny and Mary with a box of tissues extended. "Yeah, right. We all know better than that. Stick some of these in your bouquet."

"Good idea." Sophia pulled a few tissues from the box then leaned forward to embrace Joy. "Thank you for everything you've done since you've arrived. I couldn't have accomplished this without you."

"Anything for you." After the rehearsal lunch the day before, they'd returned to Sophia's so her friend could pack luggage for the honeymoon. Joy had spent the time gathering everything they'd need to bring to the wedding venue today. Of course, during the packing, Sophia had demanded to know the reason for Joy's smudged mascara—the woman was way too observant—and Joy had spilled everything. At least she'd managed to reign in her tears that time.

"You look absolutely amazing." Ginny pushed

forward in her ice-blue lace, empire-waisted gown. "Like the perfect chocolate truffle layer cake. Ooo, or better yet, a black-tie cheesecake with a raspberry topping. Elegant and classic but decidedly delicious."

"Uh, thank you?" Sophia's laugh sounded like tinkling glass as she embraced Ginny.

Mary, who was six feet tall but not intimidating in the slightest, slid a final bobby pin into her blond updo. "Now you're just making us all hungry."

"Good thing your family is catering today, then, because it means we're in for the best food ever." Sophia lowered herself daintily onto the edge of a chair.

"Between them, me as a bridesmaid, and my brother as the photographer, you couldn't have gotten married without the Hammett family." Mary slid a white faux fur wrap over her bridesmaid dress. Even though William and Sophia had rented portable heaters for the outside ceremony, Joy was grateful they'd have some extra coverage from the wind.

A knock sounded on the door of the bridal suite.

"Come in," Sophia called.

A handsome man stuck his head into the room, a camera slung around his neck. He was even taller than Mary with brown curls and the same bright green eyes as his sister. "If you're ready for photos, we can begin."

"Great, thanks, Michael."

"Sure. Would it be possible to grab the rings from you? I'd like to take some shots with them in the foreground and you and William in the background."

"Of course." Sophia turned to Joy. "Where are they?"

"They should be in the box with all the other things we brought with us today." Joy strode to the back corner of the room where she'd placed the box. Though it was normally the best man's job to hold on to the rings, William's brother Garrett hadn't been available to participate in the pre-wedding festivities. When Joy had volunteered to be in charge of the rings instead, the bride and groom had gladly agreed.

The box was kind of tall, so Joy had to strain to see into it. She sifted through the contents—a sewing kit, stain-remover wipes, breath mints, pain relievers, floss, extra buttons, deodorant, and more—and was about halfway done before a slow panic built inside her.

She remembered grabbing the rings and placing them on the dresser when she was gathering items the day before. But had she actually placed them in the box?

Or had she been too distracted by her break-up with Oliver that she'd forgotten?

"No." The word whooshed out and clanged an invisible bell that signaled doom.

"What's wrong?" Sophia appeared at her side.

Joy's hand skimmed the bottom of the box for the third time but didn't come up with anything else.

She'd failed her best friend. How was this possible?

"Joy? Are you okay?" Sophia's gentle touch was way nicer than Joy deserved.

Determined to stand her ground though faintness threatened, her eyes flitted to Sophia. "I forgot the rings."

Sophia's jaw went slack.

"I'm so sorry, friend. I can go get them—"

"You'd never make it back in time." Sophia chewed her bottom lip, leaving imprints in the red color. Her friend bravely straightened her shoulders and visibly shook off the concern. "It'll be fine. We just won't do the ring exchange part, or maybe we can find some twisty ties or something like that."

"On it!" Ginny took off out the door and down the hall, presumably toward the kitchen.

Sophia deserved so much more than twisty ties for rings. She didn't even have her engagement ring to show off because she'd chosen to have it soldered to the wedding band the week before.

How could Joy have allowed herself to become so inattentive to the people who mattered most in her life? First, she'd failed Mom. Now her best friend.

This was a disaster.

"Don't worry." Sophia tilted her head and smiled.

"There are bound to be things that go wrong today. But remember—in the end, I'll be William's wife, and that's all I care about."

Dad had tried to soothe Joy too, telling her that Mom's escape and fall were almost inevitable at some point. That was one of his arguments for moving to the assisted living facility—so the likelihood of future occurrences would be lessened. But Joy had shut that down, reminding him Mom had always valued family and home and that staying together had to be a top priority.

Oliver's words from their conversation on Christmas Eve floated back to her. *I started to see myself as some kind of savior. . . . I thought it was solely on my shoulders to save my employees from ruin the way I'd been ruined years before that. But it wasn't. Because I forgot to factor in God.*

Was Joy doing the same, inserting herself into a role she wasn't meant to play?

But employer and daughter were different things. A daughter was forever. And yes, she needed God's help in caring for her mom, but she also recognized that God wasn't going to just provide another way. *Joy* was the way he was providing.

"Joy? It'll be fine, okay?"

She forced a smile at Sophia's words. "Okay."

But she knew that wasn't true. Not one bit. And as soon as she had a chance, she'd do what she could to right the wrong she'd committed against her friend.

IF SHE TIMED it just right, she'd be able to get to Sophia's and back before her friend departed for the honeymoon.

Joy swiped the mascara sure to be dripping from her eyes and headed toward the ballroom's exit. She'd just delivered the sappiest of all maid of honor reception speeches, leaving both her and Sophia in tears. Now the dancing was in full swing as the bride and groom made their way around the room to greet guests.

Stopping a moment, Joy turned and peeked back at her best friend. Sophia was radiant standing next to William, who looked dashing in a peak-lapel tuxedo and simple black silk bowtie. The way he only had eyes for his bride, whose laugh fluttered through the manor's ballroom as she clutched a flute of non-alcoholic cider and talked with abandon— well, Joy's heart nearly burst at the sight.

But then her attention caught on the hand holding Sophia's drink. Instead of a gorgeous princess-cut diamond that should have reflected the holiday lights strung from the ceiling, her ring finger featured a red twisty tie from a bag of bread Ginny had managed to locate in the kitchen just minutes before the ceremony.

The audience had laughed along with the bride and groom as they'd twisted them onto each other's fingers, joking about never taking them off. But the entire time, Joy's gut had roiled, her face flaming. It had been difficult to push aside her guilt and enjoy the sacred ceremony, even her two favorite parts—when Sophia had cried as she'd walked down the aisle toward the man she loved, and when William pledged to love and care for Sophia.

And if that hadn't been enough to make Joy sick to her stomach, she'd spent the entire wedding thus far avoiding Oliver—first his gaze, which had tried to catch hers more than once throughout the ceremony, and then his presence during the reception, when he'd attempted to talk with her. Fortunately, as maid of honor she had several duties to perform, so she had plenty of excuses for not having time to chat.

Focus, Joy.

Right. She left the noise of the hundred or so guests and classic love songs like "My Girl" behind and entered a hallway that eventually led to steps converging with another set of stairs to form the grand staircase.

Amid the goings-on, she'd formulated a plan—slip out after speeches, borrow Ginny's car, get the rings from Sophia's house, and return before the newlyweds left. She'd miss the cake cutting, but she hoped Sophia would be too busy to notice her absence.

From the bottom of the stairs, a man approached. Oliver. Seeing him again—especially in his tux, ice-blue vest, and matching straight tie, his hair and beard trim and neat, his eyes sparkling with concern—nearly collapsed her lungs. He stopped just shy of her, putting them momentarily at about the same height.

"I'm sorry, but I don't have time to talk. I've got to go." She picked up the hem of her gown and continued past him down the steps. "I have to get those rings to Sophia and William before they leave for their honeymoon."

Oliver caught up to Joy and matched her pace. They reached the foyer, where tall tapestries decorated the walls and sconces lit the cavernous space filled with columns and grandeur. "They're staying at a B&B tonight then flying out to Italy early in the morning. They won't have a chance to swing by home on their way to the airport."

"But—"

"Ginny said I could borrow her car. I know I don't have any driving experience here, but it's mostly a small road and not too far. Daylight is almost gone, but I've driven at night plenty of times, so I'll be good."

"Joy."

She zipped her parka over the blue dress, preparing to face the cold. "I'm sorry, Oliver, I have to go."

But his hand on her arm halted her midstride. "If you'd just listen for a moment, there's something I need to tell you."

"Sophia has to have those rings. They can't go off on their honeymoon without them. It wouldn't be right." Turning, she finally allowed herself to peek up at him. Mistake. His warm gaze nearly drove her into his arms. How she wished she could hide there. But she was a grown woman who needed to buck up and handle her own problems. She'd made a mistake. And she'd set it right. "She deserves perfect. I already screwed that up for her wedding, but I can at least make sure her honeymoon starts off on the right foot. She needs those rings."

"I agree."

Joy tugged out of his grasp. "Then why are you trying to stop me?"

A smile slid easily across Oliver's lips. "If you'd let me get a word in, you'd know."

"Sorry." She blew out a breath and crossed her arms over her chest. "What are you trying to say?"

He stuffed his hand into his pants pocket. "I have the rings."

"What?"

He produced the two circular objects, and Joy nearly yelled in exultation.

"My parents arrived in Port Willis this morning, so when I heard the rings had been left behind, I called them. My dad drove them down as soon as he could. I was just coming from the parking lot to give them to you." Holding the rings out to her, he waited until she opened her palm. Then he dropped them in.

The metal felt cool as her fingers curled around them. She'd better stick them in the pocket of her jacket for safekeeping. "But how did he get into Sophia's house? How did he know where they were?"

"My aunt has a key for emergencies. I asked William, and he asked Sophia where she thought they may be. He was only there a handful of minutes before locating them."

"I don't know what to say." Though her mind was spinning, her mouth couldn't keep up. "I guess we should head back up."

Oliver followed along as she made her way to the ballroom.

But just before re-entering the wedding, she turned. "Thank you."

"Of course. I care about William and Sophia too. And you." For a few moments, Oliver just stared at her. "I knew you'd try to sneak away. And that Sophia cares more about having you here than having her ring."

Even after less than two weeks, he knew her well.

He continued. "You know that, right? People don't want you around simply because you do nice things for them or help them out. It's because you're you. You light up every room you're in. You live up to your name more than anyone I've ever known."

She sucked in a quick breath. How was she supposed to leave him standing here, pretending indifference?

From inside the ballroom, "Unchained Melody" began to play. One of her favorites. So soulful, so full of longing. It fit her mood perfectly right about now. "Dance with me?"

Without breaking eye contact, he took her hand and led her inside. Then, after helping her out of her parka, his gentle tug brought her with him to the dance floor. Taking her right hand in his left, and placing his other around her waist, he pulled her close.

She leaned into him, the wool of his tuxedo jacket surprisingly soft against her cheek. They fit so well together—and not just in the way their bodies moved fluidly around the dance floor, but also in the way he'd come to her rescue without her even asking him to. The way he'd anticipated her moves and decided to act in aiding her.

Simply put, he'd become her hero when she hadn't even been looking for one.

And that was the best kind.

"Joy?"

"Hmm?"

"I didn't get a chance to tell you how smashing you look tonight. Simply gorgeous, love."

Do not look up, do not look up, do not look up.

If she did, she'd be a goner.

Not that she wasn't already. But the fragile seam holding her heart together would finally break completely if she let him kiss her again.

"Thank you," she mumbled. Joy forced her eyes to roam the room, at the other couples swirling around them.

There were Mary and her husband, Blake, dancing comfortably and talking.

And Ginny and Steven, heads together, smiling.

Nearby, William twirled Sophia and dipped her then leaned in for a kiss.

Pop. There went a stitch. Joy tightened her hold on Oliver's hand and he did likewise. She closed her eyes and allowed herself this moment.

Pop. Another.

The song ended more quickly than she'd hoped, and the DJ replaced it with something upbeat. Despite the change in pace, Oliver kept rocking Joy back and forth for a few moments longer. He must know what she did—this was their last chance to be together.

Her heart hung on by a thread.

Groaning, Joy pushed herself from his arms. "That was great. Thank you."

"Joy—"

"I . . . can't." Holding in a sob, she maneuvered around guests and raced to her jacket. She had to return the rings before she completely lost her mind and focus.

But as she felt in her jacket pocket for the rings, her phone vibrated against her hand. Tugging it from the inner pocket, she studied the screen. She'd missed a call from Dad. And he'd left a voicemail.

It was probably nothing. But why, then, did she have this sinking in the pit of her stomach? Cold dread wrapped itself around her heart, jerking at the last stitch holding Joy together.

With her jacket flung over one arm and her phone clutched in hand, she hurried from the room to the relative quiet of the hallway and pressed the button to listen to her voicemail.

Dad's voice filled the line. *"Hi sweetie. I don't want to worry you, but your mom has developed pneumonia. They're going to keep monitoring her here and move her to the hospital if she gets any worse. I'll keep you informed about what's going on when I know more. Love you. I hope the wedding is going well."*

Pneumonia? People died of pneumonia, especially the elderly. Especially those with weakened immune systems or those in hospitals.

She dialed Dad's number, but the call went to voicemail. "Dad, it's me. Call me when you get a chance. I have a few questions about Mom."

What now? She wasn't supposed to leave town until Monday, but she couldn't wait around while Mom suffered. Who knew the severity of her condition?

The rehab center. They'd know how Mom was really doing. Joy dialed and the front desk connected her to Mom's nurse, Linda. Joy's voice shook as she asked the question she feared speaking aloud. "Linda, hi, it's Joy Beckman. How is she?"

"Tolerating treatment at the moment. Sleeping when she's not coughing."

"She's stable, then?"

"Yes, but you know how quickly someone can turn."

"Okay, thanks, Linda."

"I'm sorry I can't give you a more definitive answer."

"It's all right. I'll be there as soon as I can."

As she ended the call, Joy shoved the phone back into her jacket and snagged the rings from the other pocket. Then she hauled herself through the ballroom doors again and scanned the room, spotting Sophia talking to her mom and Ginny.

Her heels clicked on the wood floors as she crossed as fast as her short legs would carry her. Upon her approach, Sophia's smile flattened. "What's wrong, Joy?"

"My mom. Pneumonia. Too early to tell what's going on. But . . ."

"You need to go."

Joy's chest heaved from the exertion of almost running in three-inch heels. And there was the emotional exercise too, what with her insides flipping all over themselves. "I don't want to abandon you."

"You're not." Sophia drew Joy into an embrace. "I love you. You're the best friend a girl could ask for. I'm so glad you were able to share this day with me."

"Me too."

Sophia released Joy. "Now go."

"I can drive you if you need me to," Ginny said. "Unless you'd rather have Oliver do it. I'm sure he wouldn't mind."

"No." That would just be . . . too much. "I'd appreciate that, though I'd hate to pull you away from here."

"The most important thing is you getting back to your mom." Sophia placed a hand on Joy's arm and squeezed.

"Thanks, friend. Oh! I almost forgot." She opened her palm and held out the rings.

Sophia let out a joyous gasp. "Where did you get those?"

"Oliver."

Her friend's brows knit together. "Are you sure—"

"Yes. I'm sure." After so many years of friendship,

she knew what Sophia was thinking. "Mom needs me. And I have to let him go."

Pop. The last stitch burst. Joy hurried from the room before she could ruin Sophia's happy wedding with her sobs.

CHAPTER 14

She couldn't remember ever feeling so exhausted or emotionally spent.

Joy stood outside her mom's room at the skilled nursing facility, fingers trembling as her hand hovered over the door handle. Why couldn't she make herself go inside? Maybe because she didn't know what she'd find. That Mom was still here and not in the hospital should be a good sign. But what if the facility hadn't been taking good care of her while Joy had been gone? Was Dad enough of an advocate? This place had the best reviews of any of the skilled nursing facilities in the area, but . . .

Just go in, Joy.

Inhaling as deeply as she could manage, she pushed open the door. The room was on the dark side, the evening sun barely peeking through the window. As Joy approached the bed, her legs wobbled from exhaustion. Thank goodness she'd taken the time to change into comfy clothes and flat shoes at Sophia's house before taking off for the airport last night. Of course, she probably smelled like airplane and no doubt her expertly applied wedding makeup had worn off. Plus, her leftover curls were probably as flat as a savanna by now.

But Joy hadn't been able to reach her father at all since he'd left that voicemail, so she'd come straight here from the airport.

As her eyes adjusted to the dimness, she could make out her mother lying in bed, eyes closed. A cough erupted from her lips, and she fidgeted, moaning.

"Mom." Joy rushed forward.

"JoJo?" Her dad spoke from the chair next to the bed. He reached beneath his glasses to rub his eyes. "What are you doing here? I thought you weren't supposed to be home yet."

"I got your message and hurried back."

A frown marred his normally jolly face. "You didn't have to do that. I only meant to keep you informed. Your mother—"

"Needed me."

Her dad studied her, frowning. "Let's go into the hallway so we don't disturb her."

With a glance back at Mom, Joy followed Dad out of the room. Her tired eyes ached against the glare of the bright fluorescent lights. She and Dad made their way into the unoccupied waiting room at the end of the hall. A TV hanging on the wall crackled with the evening news. On a side table in the corner rested a Charlie Brown Christmas tree decorated half-heartedly with a few tiny red bulbs.

"She's fine, JoJo. The antibiotics are working and she's responding."

"That's good to hear." Joy's muscles protested as she plopped into a not-so-comfortable seat. "I know how bad pneumonia can be, and when I couldn't get ahold of you, I came as quickly as I could."

Dad sat next to her. "Did you miss the wedding?"

"Only the last few hours of the reception. Sophia understood."

But did Oliver?

She couldn't think about that now, about how she'd left without saying goodbye. Was it duty or fear that had led her to do such a thing?

Maybe a bit of both.

Joy hurried on. "But I'm back now and things are going to be different than before. You guys have my full focus again. During the plane ride, I started researching how we may be able to get a little more help with Mom at home. That would give us both a bit of a break from caregiving on a regular basis, which would allow us—"

"I've decided to move."

A distinct buzzing filled Joy's ears, and it had nothing to do with the television meteorologist reciting the weather report for the following day—sunny with a high of seventy-four.

She must not have heard him right. "Come again?"

His features softened and he leaned his head back against the white wall. "The Glenn River facility. I showed you the pamphlet, remember? They have an immediate opening, and I've decided to take it for your mother and me. We can live together in the same apartment. It's often difficult to find a situation like this, especially one as affordable as Glenn River."

He couldn't be serious. "But Dad, you don't have to spend the money. You have me." Joy gripped the wooden armrests until her fingers pulsed and pressed white.

Dad placed his hand over hers.

He was putting on a brave front, Joy could see that. There's no way he could actually want to leave the house he and Mom loved and move into a tiny apartment. To have strangers inside his home every day, multiple times a day. To give up the life he knew.

"I'm sorry." A tear slid down Joy's nose as she bent forward in her chair, placing her elbows onto her knees, her head into her hands. "This is all my fault."

"What are you talking about?"

"If I hadn't fallen asleep, let Mom leave the house unattended . . ."

"JoJo, look at me."

"No." She couldn't bear to see the pain in his eyes.

Dad sighed and ran his hand down her back in light circles like he had so many times when she was a child. "I was already considering the move before your mother broke her hip. You know as well as I do that it would have eventually come to this, that we wouldn't be able to care for her at home for the rest of her life. It has nothing to do with you and your capabilities. Having you here has been so helpful—you'll never know how much—and we've made some wonderful memories this year. But it's time to let someone else carry the burden."

Her head popped up. "Mom's not a burden."

"No, but caring for her is. One that you were never meant to take on your shoulders forever. And it could be a long road yet."

"But I'm her daughter."

"And I'm her husband. In sickness and in health, until death do us part, remember? This is my life, and this is my choice. I choose to be with her, for as many days as we have left together. That may be ten months, or it may be ten years. No one but the good Lord knows. But you still have your whole life ahead of you. In the moments when she's lucid, she's told me that she feels awful that you've thrown away your career to be here with her. And she doesn't want you throwing away your chance at happiness, whatever that may include."

"I'm not throwing anything away." Oliver's face flashed in Joy's mind, which only made her chest tighten more. "This is my life and my choice too, Dad. I don't want to have any regrets."

Then why did you leave him without saying goodbye?

She nearly growled in frustration. Why couldn't her inner voice just take a day off for once?

Joy stood and wiped the moisture from under her eyes. She steeled her petite frame. "I need to see Mom again. Once she's past this pneumonia business—and I'm not dead on my feet after nearly a day of travel and no sleep—we can discuss this like two rational adults."

Then she charged down the hallway toward Mom's room before Dad could get out another word.

CHAPTER 15

The whole world was preparing for the start of something new. Why couldn't Joy get on board?

She walked the brick pathway winding along the banks of the river in downtown New Port Richey, which was just up the road from the skilled nursing facility. Having spent every waking moment in her mom's room since she had arrived the day before, she'd finally stepped outside for some air.

And as she passed the facility's front desk, that's when she'd remembered—tomorrow was New Year's Eve. The day after that, New Year's. A time for making resolutions. For welcoming change.

Joy didn't want to do either one. She wanted to keep things exactly as they were.

But why?

Inhaling the scent of steaks cooking on a charcoal grill nearby, Joy meandered the path, passing plenty of couples and families taking advantage of the seventy-degree weather. No need for a parka here, just a linen long-sleeved red blouse, cuffed jeans, and white Keds. In grassy areas beside the river, people biked, tossed Frisbees, and picnicked under the sycamore and redbud maple trees. Nearly every bench along the path was filled.

Her phone rang from her back pocket. Joy nearly fumbled it in her rush to remove it. As she glanced at the Caller ID, she did a double take and answered. "Uh, excuse me? You're only two days into your honeymoon. Why in the world are you calling me?"

Sophia laughed. "Well, hello to you too."

"Sorry, I was just so shocked to hear from you." Joy let up on the teasing. "Everything okay?"

"Oh, yeah. Great, in fact. Italy is absolutely breathtaking. There's so much history here in Rome."

"I can't wait to hear all about it. When it's over. Does your husband know you called me? I'm surprised he doesn't want you all to himself right now."

A man with Oliver's build walked toward her, a leashed dog beside him. The terrier barked at Joy as they passed.

She sped up.

"It was his idea." Joy could picture Sophia sticking out her tongue in that playful way that only her closest friends ever saw. "I know we've texted a bit, but I have a few minutes before we head out to dinner and wanted to check in. How's your mom? How are you?"

Joy released a breath and some tension from her shoulders with it. "Mom's doing good, actually. Much better than I thought she'd be. In terms of the pneumonia, anyway." The confusion seemed to be at an all-time high—or maybe Joy had just forgotten in her nearly two-week absence how bad things really were. So far, Mom hadn't recognized her once since she'd come home. It had been all Joy could do not to break down at the polite distance in her eyes. "And me . . . well, I'm hanging in there. Dad decided to move them into that assisted living and memory care facility once Mom's released from rehab, so I'm currently devising ways to convince him that he's making a mistake."

Her friend grew silent on the other end for a few moments before speaking again. "Is he, though?"

"Soph, we've talked about this."

"I know, but . . ." Sophia sighed. "Never mind. Have you gotten any job leads?"

"No." The temptation not to tell the whole truth came and went. "To be honest, I unsubscribed from the job alerts."

"Why?"

"I can't pretend that my reasoning is entirely well thought out. It may have occurred yesterday after my dad told me his decision." She'd been so emotional, so determined to do her part in clinging to the future she knew to be right.

"Ah."

"Don't 'ah' me."

"Like you haven't had many, many occasions to 'ah' me over the years."

"Older, wiser, remember?" Joy stood aside for a mom pushing a double-wide stroller along the path. The woman thanked her, and Joy continued on her way to, well, wherever she was going.

A metaphor for her life, perhaps?

"Joy, in all seriousness, though . . . how are you feeling about being there? About leaving England?"

The question hung between them for longer than it should have. But Joy simply didn't have an answer. "I'm trying not to think about it."

"That won't work for long."

"I know." She spied an unoccupied bench and stopped walking. Sliding onto it, Joy stared out across the river. A kayak glided by, paddles piercing the sparkling water. "How was he?"

"Oliver?"

"Yeah."

"You sure you want to know?"

"No. And yes." Her teeth nipped the inside of her lower lip, and the metallic taste of blood collided with her tongue.

"He was devastated, Joy. He couldn't believe . . ."

"That I didn't say goodbye?"

"Yes. And, I think, that it was really over." Sophia exhaled. "I know you told him you didn't see a future together. But I think he hoped you'd change your mind somehow."

"But I had to leave."

"Except . . ."

Joy straightened. "Except what?"

"Well, your mom was actually okay, right?"

"I didn't know that at the time." She sounded defensive, yes, but really. After all that Joy had been through with her mom, Sophia had no right to doubt her decisions.

"True—and I would have probably done the same thing. It's just that . . ."

"Spit it out, Sophia." Oh, hostility wasn't a good look on her, but in a way, it felt good. "How would you have handled *your* mom being sick? I know it's hard to imagine since she's never had any health-related issues, but please, tell me how I *should have* behaved."

The quiet on the other end told Joy she'd gone too far.

"I'm sorry, friend. I know you love me." She groaned and closed her eyes momentarily as she massaged her forehead. "What were you trying to get through my thick skull?"

"I *do* love you, and that's the only reason I'm saying this." Sophia's voice shook.

Joy had spoken to her friend on the phone enough to know she was on the verge of tears. Guilt welled up in her throat.

"I'm just wondering if you being there with your mom has actually done anything to help her recover more quickly."

The gentle words carried with them a force that left Joy feeling slapped. "I guess not but it's only been a day. And even if it hasn't helped her, it's helped me to be close. Being away from her right now would be torture."

"Why, though?"

What was Sophia getting at? "Because I love her."

"Of course you do. That's not the issue. That's never been the issue. You love more fiercely and more completely than anyone I know. You hear someone you love is in trouble and make a snap decision to drop everything and help them."

"And there's something wrong with that?"

"No. But I think you sometimes assume that you're the only one who can help."

"That's not true." Right? "I just have a lot less going on than other people. More time available to help. No spouse, kids . . ."

"Is that why you couldn't let yourself accept the possibility of something with Oliver? Because you'd have to sacrifice the ability to help others? Do you think that just because I'm married now means I no longer can be there for those I love?"

"Of course not."

"Then maybe fear is what really stopped you from being with him."

"You have no idea how much it killed me to walk away from him." Joy couldn't sit anymore. She hopped up and pumped her legs as she headed back toward the nursing facility. Sophia's words—however lovingly spoken—pummeled her. But no matter how quickly she moved, she couldn't outrun them. "What do I have to be afraid of? The worst has already happened. I lost him."

"I'm so sorry, friend. I'm not trying to add to your pain."

"I know." Joy swallowed a few sobs. Ugh, she was so tired of crying. The last year had probably produced more tears than all the rest of her life combined.

"But think about it. It's less scary to choose your parents over Oliver. There's no risk of potential heartbreak. And you figure you have the backing of the Bible, right? The idea of 'putting others before yourself'? You don't even have to consider whether you made the right decision because it's ultimately God's will for us to help others."

"Isn't it?"

"Yes, but I think sometimes God wants us to be stretched. To choose the thing that's frightening and unsure. To live boldly. To take a chance on the unknown."

"I understand that. I do. But I can't just abandon my parents, even if Dad wants me to."

"It's not abandoning them to have a job and a relationship. And it's what your parents want. Don't they get a say in their own lives? Or do you think that you know better than them?"

Joy opened her mouth to protest, but stopped herself—because yes, without realizing it, that's exactly what she'd thought.

"And besides all of that, don't you trust God to take care of those you love without you?"

Joy huffed into the phone, her breath coming in short bursts as the questions drilled closer and closer to her heart. "I don't know, Sophia. I don't know anything anymore."

Except she did.

Joy Beckman knew two things—that she loved her parents with all her heart and that, if given the chance, she could feel love of a different sort for Oliver Lincoln.

TWO HOURS LATER, Sophia's words still rattled around in her brain. *Don't you trust God to take care of those you love without you?*

Joy sat in the wooden chair next to Mom's bed while she slept, laptop balanced on her propped legs. The cursor hovered over the SUBSCRIBE button.

Should she sign up for job alerts again? Stop fighting Dad's decision? Willingly and graciously give up her role as Mom's caregiver?

For so long, she'd known her place. Was God asking something different of her now?

Without making a decision, Joy groaned and shut her laptop then glanced at Mom. She had more color in her cheeks and was already coughing less than she'd been the day before—and apparently a lot less than earlier this week. Everything she'd seen indicated that the nursing staff had done a fabulous job of caring for Mom in Joy's absence.

Mom's eyes drifted open as Joy contemplated Sophia's words further. Joy shouldn't stare at her—her mother tended to get flustered under others' watchful gazes if she was having a less lucid moment when she awakened—but she couldn't help it.

"Hi, sweetie. Why the long face?"

Sweetie. Did Mom recognize her at last? Joy swallowed the lump in her throat and put her laptop aside. "It's nothing, Mom. How are you feeling?"

At Mom's push of a button, the bed lifted to sit her upright. "Much better, I think."

"You seem like it." Joy snagged Mom's cup off her movable side table. "Here's some water."

"Thank you." Mom took it from her hand and sipped through the tiny straw. "What were you doing on the computer? Something for work?"

It wasn't worth it anymore to point out her mother's lapses in memory. "Kind of."

"How was the wedding, dear? You haven't shown me photos yet."

Actually, she had, but Joy grabbed her phone anyway and swung her chair closer to Mom.

"Why don't you climb up here with me? It'll be easier to see them."

"Really?" The last time she'd snuggled in bed with her mom, it hadn't been two minutes before Mom had freaked out about a stranger lying next to her. But in this moment, Joy craved the closeness. "Okay." She settled into the spot beside Mom then navigated her phone to photos of her time in Port Willis.

Just like she had the day before, she flipped through the photos, skipping quickly over one of her and Oliver in front of Sophia's Christmas tree. Oliver had plopped a Santa hat onto Joy's head, taken her phone, and kissed her cheek while snapping the selfie. The goofy grin on Joy's face said more than words ever could.

"Who was that?"

"Uh, no one."

Mom looked down her nose pointedly at Joy. "Sweetie, that wasn't no one. That was an attractive man giving my daughter a kiss. One she seemed to enjoy very much."

My daughter . . . The words were sweeter than any of the treats Ginny had made last week. If only this moment could last forever. "It doesn't matter, Mom." Joy leaned her head on Mom's shoulder and inhaled the scent of her eucalyptus mint shampoo. Being here, with her—that's what mattered most.

"Of course it does."

Joy couldn't hold in the tears any longer.

Instantly, Mom wrapped her thin arms around her daughter, and Joy clung to her, burying her face in Mom's embrace. No longer was she a forty-two-year-old woman, but a little girl with a scraped elbow, a middle schooler who'd been teased, a teen who'd failed. Regardless of how much Mom forgot about her life and who she was, no matter how feeble and withdrawn she became, she'd always be the wiper of tears, the encourager of dreams, and the best woman Joy knew.

Joy would keep holding onto that and to moments like these—when Mom was just Mom.

"Shh, there, there, baby. Whatever it is, nothing's so bad the sun won't shine tomorrow."

"But it is, Mom. It is." And the entire story poured from Joy's soul—every last detail, even the ones she probably should have filtered out. But she didn't know how to be the one taking care of her mom anymore. And perhaps it was selfish, but right now, she wanted someone to take care of her.

"Oh, my darling girl." Mom pulled back so she could look into Joy's eyes. Hers were shining too. "I never should have allowed you to move home."

"I didn't give you much choice. And I wanted to be near you."

Snagging a tissue off her side table, Mom used it to dab the moisture from Joy's cheeks. "Ultimately, that's why I let it happen. I knew I was drifting away from you little by little, and I wanted any time with you that I had left. But now I see how selfish I've been."

"You've never been selfish a day in your life."

"Well, that's a load and we both know it." Mom chuckled. "You have always been an example to me of selflessness."

"Me?" That couldn't possibly be true. She curled once more against Mom. This could all end at any second, and she wanted to soak up every bit of Mom she could before she left Joy again.

"Yes, you. You've always been my little helper, and I've taken it for granted that you would be there if I needed you." Mom gripped the tissue. "But I never wanted you to do so at the expense of your heart. Love is a gift, my darling. Don't chase it unnecessarily, but if it finds you, hold on tight. That is not a selfish thing to do. Frightening? Oh, yes. But not selfish."

"What we're feeling for each other—it's rare. And it's a gift." Oliver's voice resonated in her heart.

Joy shook her head. "I've only known him for a few weeks."

"Love has grown in far less time than that. I only

knew your father for a day or so before I realized he was the one for me. Of course, I didn't tell him that, and he didn't tell me he loved me until months later. But I knew early on."

Joy had always written off that notion, called it silly. Now, though . . . "But how do we overcome the real obstacle of living in two places?"

"Have faith. If God is calling you to this, if he is giving you this blessing, then he will make a way. You don't have to see what that way is to believe it exists."

Could it be true? Was faith enough?

Yes.

The word vibrated deep within her, and she knew what she had to do. "Mom, I have to go." Joy kissed Mom's cold cheek. "Please be here when I get back."

"I'll try, sweetie. I'll try."

CHAPTER 16

She wasn't going to make it.

Joy pulled onto High Street then let loose a tiny screech as a car barreled toward her. She jerked the wheel of the rental toward the left side of the road, where she was supposed to be. At least it wasn't snowing. The mist she'd encountered while driving from Cornwall Airport Newquay to Port Willis had been difficult enough.

Her heart beat wildly—and not just because of her near accident but because of what she was about to do.

Despite the late hour, Port Willis was more alive than usual tonight. The windows of a few popular pubs glowed as she drove past, loud music spilling from inside as patrons entered and exited. According to Sophia, Port Willis didn't host an official fireworks display at midnight, though some residents set off sparklers and smaller fireworks from their homes to celebrate bringing in the new year.

Joy glanced at the clock on the car's dashboard, which flashed 11:45 p.m. She hadn't come this far—and endured two layovers and a long wait in Newquay for a rental car—to be late. The car growled as she accelerated as much as she dared.

Finally, she turned onto the quiet street where Oliver's aunt lived. Cutting the engine, she climbed from the tiny Smart car, clutching a package in her hands. The biting chill—and the fact she'd forgotten to pack gloves—reminded her she wasn't in Florida anymore. Joy pulled her knit cap down around her ears and stared at the two-story fisherman's cottage with gray slate siding and custom hardwood windowsills.

Propelling herself forward, Joy pushed open a gate leading to an adorable courtyard. A lit Christmas tree peeked from behind thin curtains in the front window, and shadows moved in the same room.

Her tongue fastened itself to the roof of her mouth. What if he didn't want to see her? What if she was blowing this all way out of proportion, making some grand gesture, and he was in there with someone else?

Joy nearly pivoted on her booted heel, but the words of her and Oliver's favorite movie came back to her: *"None of us can see the way forward in the fog.*

We simply must take the next step and trust that the light will lead us where we need to go."

The light had led her here. It was up to her to trust.

She stood firm and knocked.

It took a few long, agonizing moments, but the door eventually opened, letting out the sound of conversation and guffaws.

A woman with a head full of white hair and a sunny smile gazed down at Joy. Her eyes twinkled in a way that reminded Joy of old vintage postcards of Santa Claus. "Hullo, dear."

She'd met Oliver's aunt only once before, when running errands the day before Sophia's rehearsal. "Hi."

Suddenly, the talking behind Mavis Lincoln ceased.

"Joy?"

Oliver.

He appeared at the door behind his aunt, eyes wide. "You're here."

"I am."

"Who's here?" A disembodied voice piped up behind Oliver and his aunt, and a sixty-something woman with shoulder-length blond hair and a clear sense of fashion snuck into the space next to Mavis.

"Uh, hi." How awkward. Now even if Oliver didn't want to see Joy, he would likely feel obligated to invite her in. She should have called or texted . . . but that never happened in movies.

Note to self—reality did not always line up with film.

"Mum, this is Joy Beckman. Joy, my mother, Tabby Lincoln."

The woman tilted her head, studying her. "Hello."

"Hi." Ugh. It's like she didn't know any other words tonight.

"For goodness's sake, let her in so she doesn't freeze," Oliver said.

Mavis chuckled. "Of course. Sorry, dear."

The two women backed away from the door as Joy stepped through.

Instant warmth settled into her bones, and the scent of pine and cookies surrounded her. The tiny room was stuffed to the brim with furniture that had obviously been clustered together to make room for the giant tree Joy had spied through the window. Tinsel and ribbon dripped from its branches, and someone had painstakingly hung hundreds of mismatched ornaments, everything from homemade popsicle photo frames, to tiny red baubles, to what appeared to be chocolate coins.

Two men—one older, one younger, both of whom looked a whole lot like Oliver—lounged on the sofa, staring at her. A woman Joy recognized as Oliver's sister-in-law hunkered over a dining table putting together a puzzle with her two young daughters.

On the coffee table sat several flutes and a bottle of unopened champagne. The family had clearly been preparing to celebrate the start of a new year together and Joy had interrupted. "I'm sorry if this is a bad time."

Oliver's entire family shifted their gazes to him, but he couldn't possibly have noticed. Not with the way his gaze remained riveted on her, a hunger burning in his eyes. "What are you doing here?"

Joy's cheeks flamed. "I came back. To talk to you." Then she remembered the package in her hand. "And to give you this."

A muscle in Oliver's cheek flinched, and he seemed to mentally shake himself from a spell. "Come on then. Let's go talk."

"No, dear, we'll leave." Mavis cast a knowing look around the room, and the rest of Oliver's family shuffled out, directing a few hurried glances back at him. His youngest niece whined about wanting to finish the puzzle.

When they were alone, Oliver stepped closer. "What's that?"

Joy swallowed. "I never got you a Christmas gift."

"Yes, you did." A tiny ghost of a smile haunted his lips.

Right, the kiss. "I got you something a bit more tangible."

"That was plenty tangible."

She couldn't help the slight laugh. "You know what I mean. Here." Shoving the package into his hands, she waited.

The thick brown paper barely crinkled as he opened it to reveal his gift. *The Fog Rolls In.*

"You said you didn't own it." On such short notice, she'd had to snag her own copy from her DVD collection. But even if all of this went badly, she liked the idea of him owning something that had once belonged to her.

"I don't."

"Well, you do now."

"Thank you."

"You're welcome."

Silence fell between them. What was he thinking?

Joy turned to the tree and fiddled with a soft angel ornament.

"How's your mum?"

"Okay, actually. I mean, the pneumonia was nothing to worry about. And my dad has decided to move them into a facility."

Oliver sidled up next to her. "Is that a good thing or not?"

"I thought there was no way it could be a good thing, but I'm coming around to it." Joy chanced a look up at him and found him already watching her. "I don't know if you've realized this about me, but I can be a bit stubborn."

"Not you." The tease in Oliver's voice brought a grin to her face.

She hip-bumped him. "I know. It's one of my many charms." Joy sobered. "But sometimes, it means I think I know what's best. And I stick to that even when others—or even my own heart—tell me differently."

"So just what are you trying to say, Joy Beckman?"

Her eyes wandered until she located a clock on the mantle. 11:57 p.m. Not much time if she wanted to do this right.

Here it went. Everything she'd been feeling the last several days spilled out of her heart and onto her lips. "I'm sorry I left without saying goodbye. And I don't know where this is going, Oliver Lincoln, but I can't stand the thought of walking away from you again. I . . . I want to take the next step, wherever it may lead us."

His arms came around her lightning fast, and a laugh bubbled from his throat. "That's what I was hoping you'd say." And he leaned down, clearly aiming to kiss her.

"Wait!" She wriggled from his grasp and looked frantically around the room before spotting a wooden chair. Joy stalked toward it and tugged it back toward a bewildered Oliver.

"What are you doing?"

"Hold on. It'll make sense in a minute." When she

had the chair positioned where she'd been standing, she climbed on it and tugged the green sprig from her jacket pocket. It was slightly squished and tiny, but it was enough.

"Is that mistletoe?" Thanks to her increased height, he now glanced slightly upward.

"It just may be." Joy placed one hand around Oliver's shoulder and leaned toward him. Then she held the mistletoe above them. "And look. We're standing under it."

The adoration in his eyes nearly melted her, but she stood her ground.

Behind them, the clock chimed midnight.

"Happy New Year's, Oliver."

"Happy New Year's, love."

Then she swooped in for the kiss she'd been anticipating—and determined that, yes, reality did indeed beat the movies.

She may not know how the next scene would play out, but if she continued trusting, continued loving, continued risking, then this was not an ending after all.

It was, instead, the most beautiful beginning.

Quick Author's Note

THANK you for joining Joy and Oliver on their journey! I hope you enjoyed it as much as I did.

If you want to meet Ginny's sister Sarah and read her love story with photographer Michael Hammett—as well as catch up with all your favorite Port Willis characters—read *Like a Christmas Dream* now!

Read on for a sneak peek...

Chapter 2: In which Sarah has decided to travel to Cornwall to help her estranged sister (Ginny!) with the opening of a new bakery...

It had been three—no four—days, but Sarah had finally arrived in the small Cornish fishing village known as Port Willis.

"I can drop you at the car park or harbor, miss. Which do you prefer?" The chauffeur she'd hired at the Cornwall Airport Newquay watched her from his rearview mirror as he idled, waiting for her answer.

"Do you know where the local bookstore is?" Sarah didn't know much about Ginny's new life, but she did know that the soon-to-open bakery was somehow connected to the bookstore she used to own with her ex-husband Garrett. According to the bookstore's website, a woman named Sophia Rose was the bookstore's current owner. "My phone is dead or I'd look it up on GPS." How she'd managed to forget her charging cord was anyone's guess. Might have been the nerves threatening to take over whenever she thought about being reunited with her sister.

"Sorry, miss. My reception isn't what I'd like. I need a new phone myself." The sixty-something man's eyes twinkled underneath his bushy gray eyebrows.

"No worries. The harbor is fine. I'm sure I can find someone to help."

People strolled along the small sidewalks past storefronts that looked to be something out of a Robert Appleton novel. Even from within the vehicle, she could feel the history in this place thrumming, a living, ever-evolving thing. Through the car doors, Sarah caught whiffs of a variety of smells all swirling together as they passed a fudge shop, a bakery, and several pubs. Raucous laughter greeted her ears as they drove by a restaurant with big windows revealing walls lined with televisions broadcasting some kind of sport.

The sun was just setting over the water as the car approached the harbor, where a handful of sailboats and dinghies bobbed.

"Here we are." The car rolled to a stop in front of a restaurant.

Sarah leaned closer to the window and made out the restaurant's name on its weathered blue sign. "The Village Pub."

"Might grab myself a nice warm supper before I head back out. Would you care to join me?"

"Oh." She'd murmured the words to herself, not expecting a reply. "That's very kind, but I need to find my sister. She lives here."

"And she didn't arrange to pick you up from the airport herself? It's only a half hour's drive."

"She doesn't know I'm coming."

"Ah, a surprise visit. That sounds lovely." The man clambered from the car and popped the trunk to the four-door sedan.

Sarah scrubbed a hand across her face. It would be a surprise, all right. Lovely? One could only hope.

But after seven years of nearly radio silence between them . . . Well, it might not be a bad idea for Sarah to get a room at the local inn, just in case Ginny's welcome was not as warm as the invitation to her bakery's opening had seemed. For all Sarah knew, Ginny had been inviting her family out of spite—to show them that she'd done what they'd all doubted she could do.

Follow her dreams and actually succeed.

The chauffeur opened Sarah's door and greeted her with a cheery smile. "Here you go, miss."

"Thank you." She took his offered hand and stepped from the vehicle. Her eyes trekked up the hill. Oops. The four-inch pumps she wore may have been her go-to for business dealings and airport travel, but they would make traversing the cobblestone street under her feet fairly challenging. At least the rest of her was properly attired with her scarf, gloves, and parka. A quick glimpse at the weather forecast a few days ago had shown an average of forty degrees, and while snow wasn't overly common in December, it did happen on occasion. But after the bitter cold snap Boston had just experienced, this was nothing.

She paid the man his tip and snagged her rolling suitcase from him. As he disappeared inside the pub, she took the opportunity to finally be alone and get her bearings. There were many lit windows down here by the water, but most seemed to be private residences. The street where she stood—appropriately labeled High Street, according to the adorable wrought-iron streetlamp—ended at the harbor and cut through the middle of town, rising, rising, rising, until it curved away from her eyes.

As she faced the harbor, Sarah got the sudden urge to climb aboard one of the boats and sail away. A breeze tickled her nose and sent strands of hair skimming across her lips. She closed her eyes and inhaled the briny air. *Courage*, it seemed to whisper. Or maybe that was her own heart, begging.

"If I had my camera with me, you'd make a pretty picture indeed."

Sarah whirled, finding a well-built man with a mop of brown curls and cable-knit sweater standing outside the pub, hands shoved into the pockets of his worn jeans. There was something so casual and self-assured about his stance, and the smile on his face only added to his small-town charm.

Of course, the way the British accent glided from his lips didn't hurt his appeal either.

And here Sarah was, gaping like a wide-mouthed fish. She straightened. "Excuse me?" The words came out sharper than she'd intended.

"I'm sorry, didn't mean to startle you." He moved a step closer and glanced at her suitcase. "We don't get many visitors in the winter months. Certainly not as many as in the summer."

"Right." She swallowed a lump that had formed in her throat. How was it possible she could stare down sharks in the courtroom, but this man she'd laid eyes on moments ago flustered her? "I'm visiting my sister, Ginny Bentley—I mean Rose. The trouble is, I'm not quite sure where to find her."

"Oh, I know Ginny. Of course, in Port Willis it's difficult to not know everyone, especially when you've grown up here." The man's easy grin unlocked a certain brightness in his eyes—which, if she were looking, she'd have to admit were the most gorgeous seafoam green color she'd ever seen.

Good thing she wasn't looking.

"Would you mind telling me where I can find her?"

"I'll do you one better. I can take you there."

She shifted, her feet pinching in the toes of her heels. "Thank you, but you can just tell me how to get there."

"It's no trouble. Actually, I've been meaning to pop in to discuss some food photography for the bakery anyway."

His comment earlier about a camera made sense now. "You're a photographer?"

He shrugged. "Professionally, only on the weekends. The rest of the time, I work at the pub." He gestured behind him. "My family owns it."

Sarah peered inside the windows of the Village Pub. Though it was only five o'clock on a Tuesday evening, the bright interior appeared fairly well filled. A fire roared in one corner, and from her vantage point, Sarah could make out a long wooden paddle and anchor hanging on the wall. "It's adorable."

"I'll tell my mother you appreciate her decor."

Sarah gripped the handle of her suitcase. "Please do. And forgive me, but I didn't catch your name."

The man stared at her for a moment before breaking into another grin. "Michael Hammett at your service."

"Sarah Bentley." She held out her hand as she would when making anyone's acquaintance.

But when he reached out, and his large hands enveloped hers, she couldn't help but think she should have allowed a breach in etiquette just this once. She shivered despite the glove that kept her from actually touching his skin.

"Very nice to meet you, Sarah. But I'm an idiot for making you stand here in the cold. Want to make our way to the bookstore?" He turned toward the steep road.

High Street, indeed. Sarah pictured snapping an ankle in her ridiculous shoes and grimaced. But it was too late to turn back now.

For the first time, he eyed her shoes. "It's not far, but I'm happy to get my car and drive you if you'd like."

"That won't be necessary. Just lead the way."

"At least let me take that for you." Before she could protest, he snatched the suitcase gently from her fingers.

"Thank you." They began the uphill trudge, and soon, Sarah's breaths came in short puffs, her toes burning. But at least she hadn't fallen. Yet.

Beside her, Michael struck an impressive figure against the night sky, where thousands of stars twinkled above them. Had she ever seen this many stars at once? Maybe at their Nantucket home, but she'd been too busy going and doing to notice.

At a break in the buildings, the cliffside opened up to a view of rolling grassy hills and a distant lighthouse that appeared to be guarding the little village nestled into the bluffs.

"Ginny doesn't know you're coming, does she?"

The abrupt question made Sarah stumble. In an instant, Michael was grasping her forearm, his hold supportive but not restrictive. Sarah couldn't help being drawn into his worried gaze. Up close, she could see a slight sheen of stubble dotting his cheeks.

"Are you all right?"

What must this man think of her, falling all over herself—and him? Sarah pulled away from his gentle grasp and forced a smile. "Thanks. I clearly wasn't planning for such a hike in these shoes."

He chuckled. "I guess you weren't."

They continued the climb, passing a few others. But the street was fairly deserted. Perhaps this was one of those small towns that mostly shut down at dusk when it wasn't tourist season.

Sarah assessed her words before speaking. "How did you know?"

"Most people don't wear heels around here."

"Not that." Sarah cleared her throat. "That Ginny doesn't know I'm here."

"Ah. Simply because Ginny isn't one for secrets and she hasn't mentioned her family coming. Considering none of us has met any of you, well . . ." He shrugged. "There would be lots of excited chatter spilling from her, I imagine."

Memories of her sister and her "chatter" warmed

Sarah's chest. "She is the most genuine person I know." And yet, Father and Mother had never seen it that way. They'd tried their best to change Ginny—to make her "more like Sarah."

She was relieved to know their efforts had been in vain.

"Here we go." Michael pointed across the street to a building that looked to be hundreds of years old—essentially like everything else in this town. Several shops lined the storefront, but the bright yellow door and the sign above it indicated which was the bookstore. The store next to Rosebud Books looked to be undergoing construction.

Sarah crossed the road and read the sign in the window: *Coming Soon: Once Upon a Time Bakery.* Her fingers twitched as she traced the letters.

Michael joined her, shielding his eyes to look inside. "Doesn't seem like anyone is here. Maybe they're at Gin's home. It's just around the corner." He led her to a quaint little cottage.

Her feet ached at this point, but not as much as her heart. Would Ginny be happy to see her, or throw her out on her ear?

Only one way to find out.

She reached out and knocked on the cottage door. The wind snickered around her as she waited. Maybe Michael sensed her anxiety, because he remained silent.

Low voices floated from inside, and finally, the

door creaked open.

The woman on the other side of the door was tall and slender, with stick-straight hair just past her shoulders and warm chocolate eyes that were older and wiser than the ones Sarah had known so well. Her jeans and Beach Boys T-shirt were dusted with flour, her feet bare.

And tears streaked Ginny's cheeks.

A redheaded man sidled up next to Ginny, slipping his arm around her shoulders. His face brightened when he saw Michael. "Hey, mate. Who's this you have with you?"

"Sarah?" The name burbled from Ginny's throat, a mix of astonishment and joy—or so Sarah hoped.

"Hey, Gin." Sarah chewed her bottom lip. "It's good to see you."

Come fall in love with Sarah, Michael, and the entire village of Port Willis in Like a Christmas Dream, Book 2 in the Port Willis Romance series, available today on your favorite ebook platform.

OR

Save yourself a little money by picking up Port Willis: The Complete Collection box set, which includes all four Port Willis sweet romance novellas.

ACKNOWLEDGMENTS

My launch team — You all are such an amazing encouragement. Thanks for helping me to spread the word about my books and for loving the town of Port Willis as much as I do.

Rachel McMillan and Melissa Tagg — Thank you for walking me through the process of indie publishing. You never made me feel bad for asking my many, many questions.

Liz Johnson — The insights and feedback you gave on an early version of this book were invaluable. Thank you also for helping me to brainstorm the perfect ending scene!

Hillary Manton Lodge — Your cover design brought Port Willis to life! Thank you for being so awesome to work with.

Marisa Deshaies — Thanks for your eagle eye and for tightening up my sometimes verbose language. ;)

Rachelle Gardner — I love having you as an agent. Thanks for all of your advice and encouragement on my first real indie project!

My family — As always, you guys rock. You stand

behind me 100% all the time, and I am blessed to have you in my corner.

And God — Thank you for the inspiration to keep writing. Even when I don't know where this journey will take me next, I know you know . . . and ultimately, that's enough for me.

Lindsay Harrel is a lifelong book nerd who lives in Arizona with her young family and two golden retrievers in serious need of training. When she's not writing or chasing after her children, Lindsay enjoys making a fool of herself at Zumba, curling up with anything by Jane Austen, and savoring sour candy one piece at a time.

She also writes sweet romantic comedies (same sweetness, same heat level!) under the pen name Kristin Canary. Check out her books there at kristincanary.com.